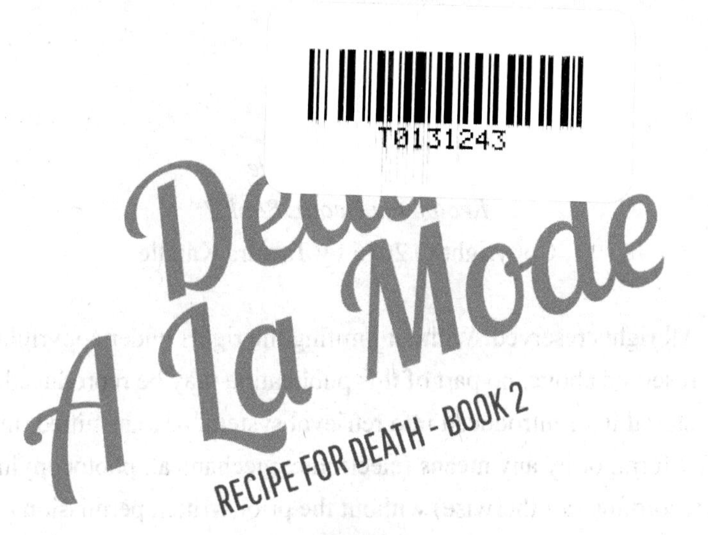

TAWDRA KANDLE

Death A La Mode
Recipe for Death, Book 2

This is a work of fiction. Names, characters, places, brands, media, and incidents are either the products of the author's imagination or are used fictitiously. The author acknowledges the trademarked status and trademark owners of various products referenced in this work of fiction, which have been used without permission. The publication/use of these trademarks is not authorized, associated with, or sponsored by the trademark owners.

Cover by Once Upon a Time Covers
Formatting by Champagne Formats

ISBN: 978-1-68230-185-2

Other Books by the Author

The King Series

Fearless

Breathless

Restless

Endless

Crystal Cove Books

The Posse

The Plan

The Path

The Perfect Dish Series

Best Served Cold

Just Desserts

I Choose You

The One Trilogy

The Last One

The First One

The Only One

The Seredipity Duet

Undeniable

Unquenchable

Recipe for Death Series

Death Fricassee

Dedication

In Memory of Nana, with love

Thank you for spoiling me, for passing on to me your love of cooking and of reading and for sharing your Wonderful Pie Crust recipe. So much of who and what I am today is because of your love and attention, and I think of you and miss you every day.

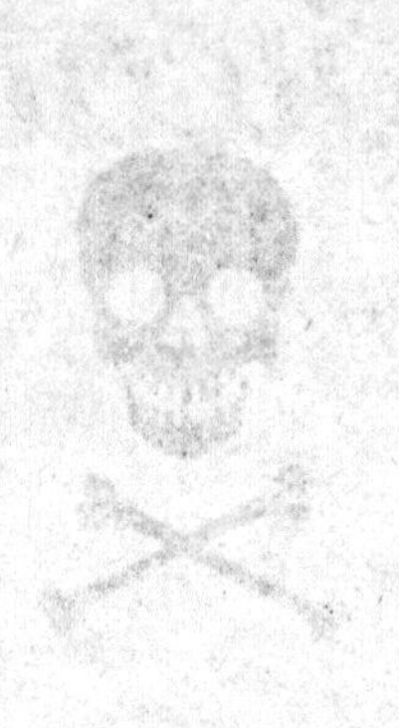

Chapter 1

"WELL, THAT WAS fun."

Lucas slid me a sideways look as he pulled the car into his driveway. "Seriously?"

"Yup." I opened the door on my side and swung my legs out, stretching from the long ride. My feet hadn't quite hit the green grass when a ball of white yapping fur attacked my ankles, small body writhing in the joy of reconciliation.

"Oh, my sweet boy. Oh, did he miss his mommy? Was he a good boy for Mrs. Mac?" I scooped my puppy into my arms, crooning to him.

"He was excellent." My neighbor and good friend, Mrs. MacKenzie, ambled toward me. "But he definitely missed his mommy and daddy."

I raised one eyebrow and smirked. "Lucas hasn't signed on as Makani's daddy figure yet, Mrs. Mac. He's not sure he can handle the responsibility. So for the time being, I'm still a single mom, struggling to make it on my own in the cold, cruel world."

"Oh, for crying out loud." Lucas popped open the trunk and reached for a suitcase. "I love the fur ball as much as you do. I just don't want to be labeled as his father. I'm more friend material."

I stood up, hoisting the dog with me. "Whatever you say. I'm taking your *friend* inside. Can you bring in my bag?"

"Sure."

Mrs. Mac walked me to my front door. "Everything go okay? You two lovebirds seem a little tense."

I forced a smile. "Oh, yeah, it was fine. You know, it was a, uh, business trip. These things aren't really for fun." I swallowed back the memory of the living room at the Carruthers townhouse. "But we're good."

"All right, honey. Well, you know, if you need to talk, I'm just next door." She patted my arm. "I'll go home now and let you get settled. Breakfast tomorrow at the diner?"

"You got it." I waited until the door closed behind her and then I set down Makani. The mail that had accumulated in my absence was piled on the kitchen counter. I flipped through it until one flyer caught my eye.

"Oh, no, she didn't."

"What's that?" Lucas dropped my suitcase onto the floor and came up behind me to read over my shoulder. "'Join us this year at the Perfect Pecan Pie Festival as Bitsy's Bites reclaims the blue ribbon!' Huh. Isn't that the pie contest you were talking about last week?"

"Yes, of course it is, and that bitch Bitsy thinks she's going automatically win it just because Al—because he's not here anymore to make his special pie? Well, she's going to be surprised when I enter a pie that blows her stupid little pastry right out of the water." I crumpled the paper in my fist. "I will *not* disgrace Al's memory by letting her win. Not while there's breath in this body." I threw the balled flyer toward the trash can, where it hit the rim and bounced onto the floor. Kobe Bryant I was not.

Lucas crossed his arms over his chest and stared me down. "Seriously, Jackie?"

I narrowed my eyes. "You keep saying that. Like there's something to talk about and I'm blowing it off."

"Oh, no, nothing at all." He shrugged. "We just got back home after we helped bring someone back from across the Divide. We brought someone back from the *dead*, Jackie. And you were possessed by a spirit, and we've just found out the end of the world as we know it is imminent. And yet you're freaking out over a pie contest?"

I blinked up at him. "The pie contest happens before the end of the world. Come on, Lucas. Learn to prioritize."

"Jackie, we need to talk about this." He raked one hand through his brown hair. "What happened to you this week—it was huge. And horrible. And fucking scary, for me at least."

"Yeah? Well, I think it's the last thing I want to rehash. For the past three days, you and Cathryn and Nell and Rafe have all been treating me like I might fall to pieces if you look at me the wrong way. And then Zoe poking at me for hours . . . it's done. Let's move on."

"We all . . . we just care about you, Jacks, and we're worried. Zoe wanted to make sure Delia didn't do any lasting damage."

At the mention of her name, I could hear her screams again, feel the clawing of her nails on my soul, as Lucas ripped her from my body. My heart pounded with the fear that she'd exuded, silently begging me not to let her go back to the gray place. Without meaning to, I winced. I turned away from Lucas, but apparently I wasn't fast enough.

"Hey, what's that?" He caught my chin and gently nudged me to look up. "What's wrong? Are you in pain?"

"Of course not." I jerked away. "I keep telling you, I'm fine. Now, can we please just get back to life in the real world?" I stooped to pick up the crumpled flier from the floor and dropped it into the trash can. "I'm going to run over to the diner for a little bit, just to check in and see that everything's okay."

"Sure." Lucas folded his arms over his chest. "Want to bring something back for dinner, and I'll meet you over here when you're done?"

I hesitated. "I'm kind of exhausted. If you don't mind, I think I'll just eat something there while I catch up with everyone, and then come home and go right to bed."

Lucas frowned, but after a silent beat, he nodded. "All right."

We stood in the kitchen for another few minutes, awkward, with neither of us speaking. I swallowed over the lump in my throat. We'd never had a real fight, only disagreements, occasional flares of snappy tempers and a day or two each month when I may have been a little difficult to be around. But now the air was heavy and uncomfortable. I was suffocating, and I needed to get out.

As if he could sense it—and maybe he could; between his vampire abilities and his death broker powers, we still weren't entirely sure of all he could do—Lucas pushed away from the kitchen counter.

"I'll be home, so if you need anything, just come over. Or yell. Otherwise I'll see you tomorrow." I noticed that he didn't make it a question. He wasn't going to let me burrow.

I decided I'd deal with that later. "Of course."

Lucas leaned forward and kissed my cheek. "Tell everyone at Leone's that I said hello."

"Will do." I stood still while he swung open the kitchen door. Turning my head, I watched him walk across the strip of grass between our houses, up the two steps to his deck and disappear through his back door.

Heaviness settled over me, and I rubbed my eyes, suddenly weary. I hadn't slept well since that afternoon at the townhouse where, together with Carruthers Initiative Institute's agents Rafe, Nell, Cathryn and Julia the necroloquitar, Lucas and I had taken part in a ritual to bring over the spirit of Delia, a Carruthers employee who'd turned out to be a traitor. For reasons that still weren't entirely clear to me, prior to her death Delia had joined with the Hive, an organization that was seeking to bring about the end of the world. Cathryn wanted to question her to see if she had information that would help in the fight to bring down the Hive.

The ritual hadn't gone as planned, unfortunately, despite Cathryn's insistence that she'd taken steps to protect us all. Instead of summoning just Delia into this plane, Nell's spell had also brought forth another dead Carruthers agent, Rafe's former girlfriend Joss. And as an added fun bonus, when Delia did make a sort-of appearance, it was inside me, the innocent bystander. She'd forced me down deep into my head, and for a terrifying time, I hadn't been able to speak or even think.

I hugged my arms around my middle and took a deep breath. Even thinking about it now made me shake. It was as though my world had turned upside down and inside out. When I'd met Lucas and eventually discovered his . . . quirk . . . of course it'd taken some getting used to. He himself was still adjusting to what had happened to him right before he'd moved to Florida, to the house right next door to mine. Through a bizarre twist of events that none of us quite understood yet, he was some sort of hybrid of vampire and death broker. His vampire half only meant that he needed to ingest blood on a regular basis and didn't like garlic. The death broker deal was more involved; it meant that he was transported to the scene of deaths, where he sent the dearly departed soul to its destination.

At first I'd thought he was insane, and then I'd gotten a front row seat to one of his death assignments. Unfortunately, it had been the murder scene of one of my dearest friends, Al Leone. The shock of losing Al had mixed with the realization that everything Lucas had told me about himself was true, and suddenly it hadn't seemed so improbable anymore. Over the past months, I'd come to accept the new dimension to my life. I'd made friends with my boyfriend's blood supplier Nichelle (it helped that I'd delivered her baby on my front yard). I kept garlic out of any dish I made for him. When I rolled over in the middle of the night and found an empty bed, I didn't freak out, since it meant Lucas had been called to a death.

Even when his mind-hearing ex-lover Cathryn, who was also his sort-of boss at Carruthers, came down to visit, I pasted on a happy face. So we hung out with a different crowd than most couples did. We double-dated with Rafe, a mind manipulator, and his girlfriend Nell, a powerful witch. Really, was I going to gripe? Before I'd met Lucas, my closest friend in the state was born during the Great Depression. It took all kinds to make the world go 'round.

But what had happened four days ago was a whole new level of crazy. The ritual, the ghost and the whole being possessed deal had unsettled me, forcing me to question everything that was going on in my life.

Well, almost everything. There was one constant in my life that always felt comfortable and right.

After their father's killer was brought to justice—in this case, justice meant a long vacation in a mental hospital in New York state—Al's family had offered to sell me his diner. Taking over Leone's had meant giving up my job as a featured food columnist for *Food International* magazine, but that hadn't been a hardship. The bigger challenge had been figuring out how not to screw up the popular Palm Dunes restaurant by making too many changes. But I was learning. And getting over there now felt like the best thing I could do. I needed a little normal.

Leone's was only a five-minute drive from my house. The diner was just outside the small over-fifty-five community where I lived as the youngest member. I'd moved in with my grandmother when she'd gotten sick, and then when she'd passed away, Nana had left me her house—with the approval of the community's board of directors, which had grandfathered me—or maybe more accurately grand*mothered* me—into the neighborhood. Something similar had happened with Lucas, though it was his aunt who'd willed him her house.

I turned my car into the small parking lot, pleased to see that it was pretty full even though it was between our normal lunch rush and the dinner run. It was true that many of our patrons tended to eat their meals a little early; Lucas joked that breakfast was served at four AM, lunch at ten and dinner at three. But still, this many customers during off-hours gave me a happy I really needed today.

When I walked through the door, familiar scents greeted me. A welcome mix of brewing coffee, garlic-infused red gravy and baking bread felt so right, so normal, that to my utter surprise and mortification, I burst into tears.

"Jackie! Welcome back." Mary, who'd started here as a

waitress decades before and now was my manager, hurried toward me. When she got closer, she frowned. "Honey, what's wrong?"

I shook my head and wiped at my cheeks. "Nothing. I don't know. I just opened the door and the smell—I guess I realized how much I miss Al. And even Nana." Sniffling, I reached for the napkin dispenser on a nearby table. "I don't know what's wrong with me."

Mary steered me to an empty booth at the back of the diner. "Did something happen on your trip?"

I dabbed at my nose, wishing I could tell Mary the truth. "No, everything was fine."

She tilted her head, studying me with narrowed eyes. "Did you and the boy have a spat?"

"No." I bit back a smile. Lucas hadn't been a boy in many a year, but to Mary, anyone under fifty fell into that category. "We're good."

"Hmmmm." She dropped her gaze to the edge of the table. "You're not . . . ahhh . . ." Mary's lips twitched. "I know I was very emotional when I was expecting."

I was confused for a second before realization dawned. "Oh, Mary, no. No, I'm not pregnant. I promise. I think it was just the stress of being away and then coming back. I haven't really been gone since we lost Al."

"That's true, hon. And I know it's hard. Sometimes I turn around from the stove and could swear I hear him giving me a hard time, asking if I put enough salt in the soup or whatever. We all miss him."

Thinking of Al in the kitchen nudged my memory. "Speaking of missing Al, guess what I got in the mail? I'll give you a hint. It was from someone whose name starts with B and ends in an 'itsy'."

"Oh . . ." Mary's eyes darkened. "That *puta*."

"Mary!" I stared at her, choking down a laugh. "I mean . . . that's not even Italian."

She groaned and covered her face. "Sorry. It's that daughter-in-law of mine. She talks like that in the kitchen at home, and she's rubbing off on me. I should know better."

"Really. If you're going to cuss, Mary, at least you need to keep it in your native language." I paused. "But you're not wrong. Bitsy's a pain in the ass, and I can't believe she'd go after the Triple P when Al hasn't even been gone a year."

"Jealous, that's what she is. Always has been. Al was good to her, offered to help her out when she opened her trashy little place, but she was snooty even then. Told him she was going to run a high-class establishment. I said to Al when I heard that, sounds like she's planning to open a brothel. He scolded me, but who was right? Jealous little thing, and now she thinks that because Al's gone, she can take over the Triple P title."

"And we don't have Al's recipe for the pie?"

"We do, but Jackie, he never followed the recipe. He added some stuff, and he never wrote it down, and I have no idea what it was."

"Damn." I folded my hands loosely on the table.

"Yeah, if there was only some way we could ask him, right?" She winked at me. "Hey, I know what, we'll have a séance and see if we can get Al to come back and tell us."

Nausea churned in my stomach. "No. Not a good idea."

"I was just kidding." Mary's forehead wrinkled. "Are you okay?"

"Yeah, sorry." I slid out of the booth. "Is there anything I need to look at before I go? Anything unusual happen while I was gone?"

"No, just business as usual. Everything's on the weekly report." Mary stood up, too. "Jackie, you know, maybe you don't have to recreate Al's pie. You're a wonderful cook. Why don't you just make up your own? You could blow that Bitsy woman out of the water."

I leaned my hand against the back of the booth. "Do you think so?"

Mary grinned. "Damned right. You're a hell of a baker. And that pecan pie'll be even sweeter when we can rub it in Bitsy's face."

"I don't have much time. The festival's only two weeks away." I chewed the corner of my lip. "I'd have to work on it almost non-stop. It'll take away from the time I can spend here."

Mary raised her eyebrows and cocked her head. "Uh-huh. Don't worry, I think we'll soldier on."

"Fine." I threw up my hands. "You don't need me. Then I'm going home to make pies."

"Give 'em hell, honey." Mary patted my back. "Baking is good for the soul."

Chapter 2

I WENT TO BED early that night, hoping to catch up on the sleep I'd missed the last few days. Just before I climbed under the covers with Makani snuggled at my side, I allowed myself a glance over to my next-door neighbor. I could see one light on in his kitchen, which meant either Lucas had gone to sleep, too, or—and this was the more likely scenario—he'd been called to a death. Either way, the house was quiet. I almost reached for my phone to text him good night, but something stayed my hand.

I wasn't angry at Lucas for what had happened at Carruthers. I knew it wasn't his fault; he'd been upset that Cathryn had suggested that I take part in the ritual at all, but they'd needed a sixth person, and truth to tell, I'd been flattered that she'd included me. I liked Rafe and Nell, and I tolerated Cathryn, but when Lucas and I hung out with them, I definitely felt . . . less. They had all these cool abilities, gifts, and I had nothing, unless you counted the ability to make a damned good soufflé. That was a gift, for sure, but not precisely a supernatural one. So the chance to be part of something they were all doing was exciting.

And there wasn't anything Lucas could've done to prevent Delia from possessing me. It happened before any of them had realized it, while the group was distracted by the appearance of Joss, who had not been called or expected. By the time Rafe had noticed me collapsed on the sofa next to him, Delia had already taken control of my body.

I knew Lucas was furious with Cathryn for letting it happen. The first thing I heard when I began to come around was him yelling at her, irate that all of her so-called precautions hadn't protected me, the weakest link. Cathryn had apologized, both to Lucas and to me, but I got the sense that she was puzzled at how upset everyone was. I guessed a simple possession was just another day on the job for the ice princess.

Still, she had insisted that I talk to Zoe. Or more accurately, that I allow Zoe to talk to me. The diminutive and colorful woman who provided counseling and therapy to the agents of Carruthers Initiative Institute had questioned me for hours about every aspect of the time Delia had held the reins in my head.

"Could you hear what was happening when Delia was in charge?"

I shook my head. "No. I felt as though I was falling—passing out, maybe—and then there was nothing. Just darkness. Silence. I wasn't even really aware."

"And then when she left? What happened?"

Sitting in Zoe's tranquil, peaceful little office, safe in Harper Creek, the headquarters of Carruthers, I gripped the arms of my chair and pushed the memory away. I couldn't deal with it, couldn't think about it, or I'd run shrieking out of Zoe's office and curl up in some corner, rocking. "Nothing happened. I came back, and I was fine. Lucas was shouting at Cathryn. They were trying to talk to Joss, I guess, about what Delia had told her. That was it."

Zoe didn't speak for a moment, but one fine eyebrow rose. I stayed silent.

"Cathryn told me that you were nearly hysterical after you awoke. She said you cried so hard, she thought they might have to sedate you."

I lifted one shoulder. "I was freaked out, yeah. Wouldn't you be?" Before she could answer, I continued. "Oh, no, I forgot, all of you are used to crap like this. Well, if this was my initiation, I guess I failed. Sorry."

"Don't be ridiculous." Zoe's tone was crisp without a drop of pity. Apparently she wasn't the coddling type. "It wasn't a test of any sort, and you didn't fail. Something unexpected happened during a relatively risky operation, and everyone feels bad that you were the one caught in the middle."

I snorted. "Yeah. 'Relatively risky operation.' Cathryn told us we'd be safe."

"And she thought you would be, but she was also upfront

with you about what was going to happen. What the goal was. There wasn't anything else that could've been done to protect you." When I didn't reply, Zoe sighed. "All right, we'll agree to disagree. Tell me how you've been the last two days. Have you been sleeping all right?"

I avoided her eyes. "I've been fine."

"You're not answering my question." Zoe smiled. "And of course there's nothing I can do to force your hand. You don't work for Carruthers, so I can't threaten to put you on a mental health hold, can I?"

This time it was me raising my eyebrows as though daring her to try it.

"Jackie, whether you realize it or not, I'm trying to help you. You went through a traumatic experience, and Cathryn wants to make sure every possible option is available to you for anything you might need. This is a safe place for you to tell me anything that's troubling you, knowing it doesn't go any further. I'm here for you, now and even after you've returned home." She opened a drawer and dug around for a few minutes, until she found an envelope, which she pushed across the desk toward me. "This is a natural sleep remedy. It won't hurt you, it won't make you sluggish the next day, and there's nothing narcotic in it. Two tablespoons to one cup of boiling water—brew it like a tea. If you can't sleep, promise me you'll at least try it."

I palmed the white square and slid it into my handbag. "Thanks. I appreciate it."

Now, lying in my warm bed at home, with a snoring pup pushed up against my side, I remembered her suggestion. That envelope was still in my purse, and the fact that I hadn't had more than a few hours of real sleep all week was beginning to wear on me. The temptation to give Zoe's remedy a try was strong, but in the end, my stubbornness was greater. Instead of brewing her tea, I climbed out of bed, stalked to the kitchen and poured myself a generous glass of white wine.

The wine didn't help as much as I'd hoped. It was nearly dawn by the time I fell into an uneasy sleep, only to be awakened by Mrs. Mac banging on my kitchen door, since I was late for our weekly breakfast.

I managed to throw on clothes and drag myself to the diner, where I guzzled two mugs of high-test coffee while my friend caught me on neighborhood gossip. It was the same-old, same-old: who was carrying on not-so-secret affairs with others in our small community, who was suspected of cheating at the weekly canasta game and whose gardens were being neglected. The nice thing was that all I had to do was nod and insert an occasional "Oh!" or "No way!"

After breakfast, I dropped Mrs. Mac at her house and headed out to the grocery store for extra flour, butter, eggs and vanilla and then to the farmers' market to buy pecans. Sleep deprivation or not, it was time to kick operation "Beat Bitsy" into high gear.

Over my years of cooking, both for my own pleasure and for my job as the cookbook columnist for *Food International*, I'd come up with an outline for developing new recipes. Following the advice of my favorite chef—that'd be my dad, who owned our family restaurant back in New York—I always began with the basics. So today, I focused on making a pared-down, no-frills pecan pie, using my aunt Tina's recipe along with my Nana's no-fail crust.

I'd just slid the pie into the oven and closed the door when my kitchen door opened. "Something smells amazing. Please tell me it's for dessert tonight."

I couldn't help smiling. I might've still been struggling with post-traumatic possession syndrome, but keeping Lucas at arm's length, especially when what had happened wasn't his fault, was impossible for me.

"It's my first foray into the pie contest trials. You arrived just in time to help with the garlic sauce I'm making for the top."

He recoiled in horror, and I laughed. He really was so predictable.

"Aww, stop that. It's not nice to make fun of your cooking-impaired boyfriend. And garlic is never a laughing matter." His faux-mad face softened into a smirk as he snagged my hand and pulled me against him. "Hey, c'mere."

For the first time since that afternoon with Delia, I let myself truly lean into Lucas, burying my head in the strength of his chest. He smelled familiar and comforting, a mix of masculine soap and some other elusive fragrance I could never pinpoint. His hands rubbed gentle circles on my back, and I sagged against him.

"You know I love you, right?" His voice was muffled as he buried his lips in my hair.

"Uh huh." I spoke against his shoulder. "I do. I love you, too."

"And you know I'd never let anything happen to you. Nothing that I could stop, if it was in my power to do it."

"I know that. I'm not mad at you. I'm not really mad at anyone. I'm just . . ." I pushed back a little so that I could see his face. "I'm a little scared, I think. Or maybe shaken up is a better way to say it. It feels like everything in the world is just slightly askew. Like I can't quite get my footing."

"I can understand that. You had a traumatic experience. Anyone would be off-kilter." He brushed the hair off my face. "I'm glad you don't blame me, but maybe you should. I keep thinking that if it weren't for me, you'd still be living a normal life. No death brokering, no vampires, no possession. No end of the world panic."

I reached up and touched his mouth with my fingertip. "No boyfriend, no love, no adventure. Lots of loneliness." I kissed his chin, loving the feel of his whiskers against my lips. "I don't like what happened this week, but I guess I wouldn't give you up in exchange for a little blissful ignorance."

Lucas raised his eyebrows. "You guess?"

"Be happy I'm talking to you, buddy. A lot of girls wouldn't be." I wriggled away from him and stuck out my tongue. "I'm just more mature and evolved."

"Sure you are." He swatted my behind as I passed. "So enough with the serious talk. Tell me about this pecan pie deal.

Why pecans? What goes on at the festival? And when can I taste the pie?"

I leaned a hip against the counter. "Ah, well, those are complicated questions, my young friend. First, it's a pecan festival because General Casey, the founder of Palm Dunes, was a pecan farmer from Georgia. He came down here with his wife to build a winter home, and he wanted to establish a new market for his nuts." I pinned Lucas with a stern look when he started to laugh. He wisely turned it into a cough. "So he started up the Perfect Pecan Pie Festival, to get people more excited about his nu—his crop."

"Okay. So it's just pie?"

I feigned shocked disapproval. "No! Oh, no. It's much more. It's music and dancing and contests . . ."

"Music? Oh, please don't tell me that means Mr. Jaegar and his barbershop quartet."

"No, smartass. It used to be a mixture of different bands, but now it's all folk music. As a matter of fact, if you must know, the Triple P Fest is one of the premier folk music events in Florida."

"Huh." Lucas looked suitably impressed. "I've been known to enjoy some folk music."

"Imagine that." I shook my head. "Actually, I'm excited because one of my favorites is going to be headlining this year. Her name's Crissy Darwin. Have you heard of her?"

"I don't think so."

I shrugged. "Well, she's just starting out. She sang at the festival the first time when she was sixteen, and she just blew me away. Now I've heard rumors that she's been offered a contract in Nashville. So I'm glad she was coming this year. Might be the last time we can see her without paying the big bucks."

"Is she local?" Lucas pulled out a kitchen chair and sat down.

"Kind of. Not to Palm Dunes, exactly. She's from Seminole Falls, about fifteen minutes south."

"Is she a fan of the pecans?"

I rolled my eyes. "I'm sure she is. More importantly, she *has* a lot of fans who come to the Triple P Fest. Including me."

"Okay." Lucas bent down from his seat and peered into the oven. "So how long does this pie need before we can eat it?"

I glanced at the timer. "About another twenty-five minutes until it's out of the oven, and then it'll need to cool, or else you'll burn the shit out of your mouth."

"Twenty-five minutes?" He stood up and slid his arms around my waist. "What in the world could we do to occupy ourselves for that long?" Dropping his lips to mine, he kissed me, at first with gentle persuasion and then with more intensity as his tongue teased my mouth to open.

But the minute it did, as soon as he deepened the kiss, panic gripped me. For a dizzying second, I couldn't breathe, and I pushed him away, wrapping my arms around my ribs and gasping.

"What is it? What's wrong?" Lucas tried to touch my back, but I shied away.

"Nothing. I don't know. I just . . . I can't. Not yet." My hands shook, and I clenched them into fists, gripping the cloth of my shirt. “I’m sorry. I felt . . . invaded. Again.”

“By me?” The hurt and shock in Lucas’ tone stabbed my heart. “Jackie, I don’t—I thought you were okay. What’s going on?”

“I told you, I’m not ready. I can’t have someone else in my body. Not again.” I forced my arms to relax and sat down in one of the kitchen chairs. “I’m sorry, Lucas. It’s not you. Like you said before, I’m still traumatized. I need a few more days.”

He studied me, not speaking at first, and I couldn’t read his expression. “Okay. I understand. I think I do, anyway.” He leaned his back against the front of the stove. “Do you want me to leave?”

I shook my head. “Not unless you want to.”

“I don’t.” He sat down across from me again. “Do you think you should talk to Zoe some more?”

“No.” I answered him quickly. “Talking to Zoe didn’t help me. And it’s not going to change anything now. I need some time. That’s all.” Unbidden, the same horrifying sensory memory of Delia being ripped away flooded my mind. I screwed shut my eyes and pushed it away.

“Are you all right?” Lucas dropped to his knees in front of me. “You just went white.” He caught my hands in his and squeezed. “And your hands are like ice.”

“Yeah.” I held onto the warmth in his fingers like a lifeline. “I don’t know, I got dizzy all of a sudden.”

“Come on.” He pulled me to my feet and wrapped an arm around me. “Come lay down on the sofa.” When I shot him a look, he frowned. “I’m not trying to start anything. I just want to make you feel better. I promise, no funny business."

"This particular sofa has some pretty hot memories." I let him lead me into the living room, where I curled up on the couch. Lucas sat down and lifted my head onto his lap.

"It does. And don't think I don't remember. But I'm capable of being a gentleman and practicing something we men like to call 'self-control'." He smoothed one hand over my hair, and my shoulders began to relax.

"If I nod off, listen for the timer on the stove. I don't want to burn my pie." My words sounded slurred even to my own ears.

"No worries, love. I got this. Just rest."

For the first time in days, I let myself slide into real sleep.

Chapter 3

"WHO KNEW PECAN pie was the perfect breakfast food?" Lucas polished off his last bite and chugged some milk. "Eggs, sugar, nuts and flour—it's got all the food groups."

I shook my head at him, smiling. "I don't think your idea of the food pyramid jives with the one the FDA follows, but whatever you say. So you liked it?"

"What's not to like?" He stole a piece of crumb from my plate. "I think you've got a winner here."

"Ha!" I moved my plate out of his reach. "This is just the opening salvo, my friend. It's a very basic version, and I'm using it to see what I need to add to make it better. Tastier.

Irresistible. Even—dare I say it—perfect."

"What're you going to change?" Lucas narrowed his eyes at me suspiciously. "The crust? I hope not, because that's delicious. So is the inside. I think it's perfect as it is."

"But it's not. It's an adequate pie for dessert at the diner. I'd serve it after a family dinner. But nothing about it screams perfect pecan pie."

"So what're you going to add? Or change?"

"I haven't decided yet. I need to play with it a little."

Lucas stretched his legs under the table. "Well, it's your lucky day. I don't have any plans today, so I can sit here and be your taste-tester."

I rose and picked up our plates, carrying them to the sink. "Didn't you tell me, right before we left for Carruthers last week, that you got the first round of edits back on your book? Shouldn't you be working on those?"

Some of the enthusiasm left his face, and he shifted in his chair. "That doesn't sound as fun as being a pie taster. I'm waiting for a delivery, too, and I can't really concentrate until I get it."

I rinsed off my plate. "I knew Nichelle was coming by. She's bringing the baby for a visit. And coincidentally, she offered to help me work on the new recipe, too."

"But I'm your boyfriend. Shouldn't I get dibs on the job?"

"Nichelle has a very well-developed palate and is an excellent amateur chef. Also, she's my friend, and she named her kid after me."

"Ah, but can she *give* you a kid?" Lucas came up behind me, sliding his arms just below my breasts, making my heart beat a little faster. Although the idea of having sex still made me panic a little, his touch made me want to melt, even as the words he'd spoken sent both a chill and a pang of regret into my chest.

"We don't know that you can." I covered his hands with mine to soften my words. "And you don't know that you want that, anyway."

He didn't move for a few seconds. "If I did, it wouldn't be with anyone but you. But until we know more about what I am, I can't risk passing on some fucked-up genetic material. Would you saddle a kid with my life? Especially in light of what happened last week? I can't even keep you safe. Why would we toss an innocent baby into the mix?"

"I know. I understand all that." I swallowed over the lump in my throat. "By the time we figure it out, it could be too late for me." Forcing a smile I didn't quite feel, I turned in his arms. "Until you came along, I'd begun to think I'd be alone forever. I'm not worried about that anymore. So I'm not going to complain. I'm going to be grateful for what I do have and not mourn what I don't."

"I hate that it has to be a choice." His voice was gruff. "If I could do it, Jackie, I'd give you everything in the world. Everything you'd ever dreamed of having. I'd give you a big white wedding and a house full of squalling babies." He wound a lock of my hair around his finger. "And so much normal, you'd be sick of it. No death, no blood-drinking, no end-of-the-world mess."

"Sounds completely boring to me." I stood on my toes and kissed him lightly. "And if you want to stay and help Nichelle as a taster, you're welcome. Just don't expect to get a word in edgewise."

Lucas grimaced. "True. I've never met a woman who could talk like her. I don't know how you ever have a conversation with her."

"She's my friend." I shrugged. "Oh, and speaking of friends, Leesa texted this morning and said something about trying to come down here for a visit over Christmas."

"Really? I'll get to meet the elusive BFF? I thought she was perpetually chained to her desk at the law firm in New York."

"Not since she and Harold got together. Now she's actually living her life. She even went to Comic Con with him."

"Wow. She's a wild woman."

"She really is. Oh, here comes Nichelle now."

It was a measure of her familiarity that my friend no longer knocked at the front door. Instead, she pushed opened the kitchen door and marched inside, nearly covered with bags and a baby.

She stopped in front of Lucas where he stood leaning against the counter and thrust a small white cooler against his chest. "Here. This is yours."

Lucas caught the Styrofoam box in both hands. "Uh, okay. Thanks."

"Hold on, let me get the paperwork." Nichelle started to dig into the stuffed baby bag on her shoulder and then turned toward me. "Take him, will you? He's a ton."

I scooped Jack off her hip. "Of course I will. Come here to Auntie Jacks. Look at this sweet boy. You're getting so big!"

Nichelle snorted. "You're telling me. I swear, every time I pick him up, he's gained five pounds." She found the paper, crumpled in the side pocket of the diaper bag, and smoothed it out on my counter. "You know the drill. Sign and initial."

Lucas took the pen she offered and did just that. Nichelle smiled at me. "I smell pie. Is that your first version?"

"Sorry, Nichelle, you're too late. I finished the last piece this morning." Lucas handed her the pen and papers. "Guess you'll have to wait for round two."

I cleared my throat, raising my eyebrows at him. "Don't you want to take your delivery over to your house and put it away?" We didn't know a whole lot about how Lucas had been turned into a half-vamp or how he differed in his needs and limitations from full vampires, but one thing had always been clear: he needed his daily dose of blood or things got dicey; he'd be distracted, fuzzy-brained and slightly short-tempered.

"Yeah, I should." Holding the cooler by its handle, he leaned over to drop a quick kiss on my lips. "I'll see you this afternoon, Jackie." Sketching a salute as he headed out the kitchen door, he added, "Nichelle. Always a pleasure."

"Yeah, yeah." She waited until the door closed behind him and then she turned to me. "Okay, where is it? I know you saved me a piece back."

Laughing, I shifted the baby to my other arm and opened up the microwave to take out a single piece of pie. "Are you sure you're not psychic? How did you know?"

"Because you're a good friend, and no matter how cute that man of yours is, you'd never give him my pie." She opened the silverware drawer and retrieved a fork. "You okay with the rug rat while I stuff my face?"

"Sure." I pulled out a chair and sat down, situating little Jack on my lap. "So tell me, baby boy, what's been going on in your life? We got some new teeths? Any new words?"

He grinned big at me and patted my cheek. "Mama!"

A stab of hurt dug into my chest, even as Nichelle sighed. "It's his new thing. Anyone with boobs is Mama. Keeps me humble, you know?" Leaning back in her chair, she took another bite of pie and closed her eyes. "This is seriously good, Jackie. Crust is light, filling has good, rich flavor."

"But . . .?" I pressed a kiss to the top of baby Jack's sweet head, and he snuggled against me.

"It's delicious, but nothing special. Nothing to make it stand out."

"That's exactly what I told Lucas." I tapped the edge of the table, thinking. "So what do I need to change to make it spectacular? What should I add?"

"It's got to be something unexpected. Like, you don't want to add chocolate. People do that all the time. Booooring." Nichelle faked a yawn.

"Okay, so no chocolate. What else could I use?"

"Pumpkin? I mean, that's seasonal." Nichelle stood up and helped herself to a glass of water.

I considered. "I've heard of pumpkin-pecan pie before. I don't think I've ever done one, though. I could try a layer of pumpkin and then the pecan on top. Or vice versa."

"Give it a shot. I'm happy to play taster." She sipped her water. "So how was your trip up north with lover boy? Did you two have a fun getaway?"

"Eh." I avoided her eyes. "It was fine. He was involved with his, uh, work quite a bit."

"Mmmhmmm." Nichelle's eyes narrowed. "And the blonde was there? She give you problems?"

"Cathryn? No. She was fine." *Except when she involved me in a ritual that let a spirit possess me.* "It was all fine."

"Do you realize you've just said 'fine' three times, talking about this trip? Which means it was totally *not* fine. So tell me what really happened."

I turned Jack to stand on my lap, bouncing him a little, just to give me a minute to think. Nichelle and I never talked about Lucas and the deliveries she made to him. She knew he got a cooler full of blood every three days, but in the months we'd known each other, she hadn't ever asked me why. If she had an inkling about what he was, she didn't give me any indication. I was aware that her business specialized in making discreet deliveries of unusual products to people who valued that service and paid for it accordingly. And although she didn't treat Lucas differently, I'd noticed that she never asked him to hold Jack. The two of them, Lucas and Nichelle, seemed to have a relationship of mutual tolerance, probably out of deference to me.

Still, since I'd never confided in her about my boyfriend's odd abilities and needs, I didn't feel comfortable telling her the whole story about our time at Carruthers. She might think I was crazy, and since she was really my own friend in town under the age of seventy, I didn't want to risk losing her.

"We just had a little disagreement. It's nothing big, and we'll be fine—I mean, we're good. You know how these things go. You've been married forever."

"True. Well, if you need someone to talk to, I'm here. I don't mean just about pie. If there's shit going down—ooops, I got to watch my mouth in front of the little sponge there. Just my luck he'll decide that'll be his second word. Anyway, if there's stuff you're thinking I might not understand, trust me. I've heard it all. And I know how to keep my mouth shut." She fluttered her hands at me. "Now gimme my kid, and you get busy on the baking. I can hang out until that pumpkin-pecan one is done if you hustle a little."

Nichelle made the ultimate sacrifice and stayed until my pumpkin-pecan pie was cool enough to taste. Jack, good kid that he was, sacked out on my bed and took a nice, long nap while his mom and I brainstormed pie ideas.

We decided that the pumpkin-pecan version was decent, a little different, but still not spectacular enough to win the contest. Between us, we came up with a list of options for me to try.

After they left, I tackled the kitchen clean-up, chatting with Mary from the diner as I cleaned. She gave me the daily report and offered me more pie-encouragement.

"Everyone at Leone's is behind you. No one likes Bitsy, and we all want to see you win. Show that little witch what's what."

"Thanks for the support, Mary." I turned as I heard the door open. "Hey, listen, I need to go. Lucas just got here, and I'm sure he wants to take me some place really romantic for dinner."

Mary laughed. "Go have fun, hon. I'll see you tomorrow."

Lucas dropped into a chair. "Did we have a date I forgot?"

"Nah, I just needed to get off the phone with Mary. And I thought I'd give you a hard time." I folded the dishtowel and hung it over my oven door handle. "What do you feel like for dinner?" We'd fallen into a fairly easy routine over the last months; though we were both more comfortable maintaining our own houses, we usually ate at least breakfast and dinner together. I did most of the cooking, of course, but every now and then, Lucas brought in take-out or made me soup. Sometimes we ate at the diner, though we tried to avoid going there too much, since it usually turned into a working meal for me, as the wait staff all wanted to chat. About once a month, we went out some place fancy, as Lucas called it, trying out local restaurants.

"Oh, I don't care. Something easy, since it looks like you've been cooking all day." He leaned forward. "Uh, Jackie, I met Crissy Darwin this afternoon."

I frowned. "You did? How? Where did you meet her?" His driveway ran between our houses, so I usually noticed when he left home. As far as I'd seen, he'd been holed up all day. I'd figured he was drinking his blood and working on the edits on his book.

"I got called out to a Reckoning."

It took a minute for that to filter into my brain, and when it did, my heart dropped. "No! Oh, Lucas, not Crissy. Tell me she's not dead."

"She's not." He took my hand and gave it a squeeze. "But her manager is. I think she was murdered."

"Her manager?" I tried to remember if I knew anything about him. Or her. When I'd first met Crissy as a teenager, her mother and father had been with her, and I'd gotten the impression they were handling her career.

"Yeah, a woman named Maddy Cane. I guess she's only been working with her for a few months. Pretty sad."

"Wait a minute." I sat down and braced my elbows on the table. "Start at the beginning and tell me what happened. How did you meet Crissy, if you were there for a Reckoning?" Moving the souls of the departed to the otherworldly realm for which they were destined was part of Lucas's death broker gig. He was transported to the scene as soon as a person died and met with two advocates, representatives for what was in essence heaven and hell, though they never used those terms.

He sighed. "Okay. I took my blood home and had a pouch of it. I'd just finished when I was transported. It was an office, but no one else was there. I saw the body, and we were handling the Reckoning when Crissy came in. She found the body."

"Oh, my God. How did you handle that? Are you a suspect now?"

He shook his head. "No. The advocates told me that death brokers always have alibis—it's part of the deal. Even if we're discovered at the scene of the crime, there's some kind of mojo that keeps us from being implicated. Which is pretty much the first good thing I've heard about this job."

"But Crissy saw you?"

"Yes. She was broken up, as you'd expect. We called the police, and so I got stuck there for a while."

"How did you explain being there? And how do you know it was murder? Was she—shot?" I had a sudden flash of my friend Al, lying dead in his own blood on the floor of the diner, and I shuddered.

Lucas stood up and drew me to my feet, holding me close. "No. At first I thought it was natural causes, but then I saw . . . evidence that maybe it wasn't. And the police seemed to concur."

"What was the evidence?" I wasn't normally a morbid person, but now my curiosity had been piqued.

"Just take my word for it. I think she was poisoned."

"Poisoned?"

"Mmmhmm. The rep from the ME's office said the same thing. Of course, they won't be able to confirm the TOD or the COD until the autopsy's done."

I rolled my eyes. "So now you're talking cop? What's next, a T-shirt under a beige blazer, sleeves rolled to the elbows and Wayfarers day and night?"

Lucas cocked his head. "I think I'm more the Columbo type than Crockett and Tubbs. Can't you see me in a trench coat, turning around to say, 'Oh, just one more thing . . .'?"

"Whatever you say." I shook my head, impatient. "Was Crissy all right? And do they know what happened?"

"Crissy was shaken up, of course. I think at first she was

in shock, and then she lost it. Oh, and if the police know what happened, who poisoned Maddy Cane, they didn't say anything in front of me."

"So they really didn't find it suspicious that you were there, just standing over the body?" I'd often wondered what would happen if Lucas were discovered at a death scene. The advocates were cloaked, as they were apparently beings who existed on a different plane, and if they were all called to a Reckoning where the dearly departed was surrounded by grieving family or hospital staff, the advocates could extend their cloaking to protect Lucas, too. But they rarely bothered to do it if they were alone.

"No. The advocate for light told me they hadn't expected Crissy to walk in, so he didn't have time to hide me. And she couldn't see them at all. But he did say that no matter what excuse I gave for being there, it would be accepted without question. He was right."

"What did you tell them?" Lucas had a good imagination, but I wasn't sure how fast he'd be at making up a plausible excuse.

"I said I'd known her briefly years ago, and since I'd recently moved down here, I wanted to say hello, so I'd just stopped in. Imagine my shock and dismay when I found her sprawled on the floor moments before Crissy walked in."

"I just can't believe it. Poor Crissy. She must be devastated. And just before she signed her contract with the music company in Nashville! I'm pretty sure Maddy was the one who negotiated that."

Lucas nodded. "I think she said something about it." He

rubbed small circles on my back. "I'm sorry about this. I realize you didn't know her, but still. Another death, even remotely connected to you, when you're still feeling unsettled . . . it's got to be tough on you."

I shrugged but let my forehead drop to his chest. "I guess when you're in love with a death broker, death becomes a way of life."

He lifted my chin and kissed me gently. "Thanks for being understanding. Now, since we've both had complicated afternoons, how about I take you over to that burger joint you love so much on the beach? We'll eat and then walk in the waves. Watch the sunset."

I lifted my eyebrows. "The sun sets on the west coast."

"I didn't say we'd watch it set over the ocean. Now go get your shoes and your purse. I'm hungry."

Chapter 4

ONE OF THE first thing I'd learned after moving to Palm Dunes to take care of my Nana was that the saying, "News travels fast" apparently had its genesis in my adopted over-fifty-five community. Word-of-mouth was a literal thing, as some of the ladies walked from house to house, sharing the latest info. They disguised their gossip mission by calling it a doctor-ordered walk, but we all knew the truth.

So I wasn't really surprised at the fast and furious information exchange the day after Maddy Cane died. Crissy herself was a favorite, as her grandparents had lived in our neighborhood before old Hank had passed and his widow relocated to live with her sister in Fort Myers. All the ladies saw Crissy as a surrogate granddaughter. Most of the men, however, had fallen under her spell; Crissy had a way of charming the old codgers so that they nudged each other, wagging overgrown gray eyebrows whenever she was around.

Mrs. Mac was at my kitchen table by eight o'clock. I was still in bed when I heard the door open and poked Lucas in the ribs.

"Hey. We have company."

"Hmmm?" He didn't open his eyes, but one arm snaked out to wrap around me and haul me close. He'd stayed over last night, even though I still wasn't ready for intimacy. Having him next to me, a warm presence in my bed, helped me sleep a little better.

"Mrs. Mac's here. I just heard the door open. I need to go out there."

Lucas groaned. "Does she have breakfast? Donuts?" And when a soft whine came from the foot of the bed, he added, "Or can she at least take out the fur ball?"

I wriggled out of his hold and stood up. "I'd say doubtful on all fronts. I'll throw on some clothes and go see what's up with her. And I'll let his majesty outside, too."

"Start up the coffee, too?" He rolled over and buried his face in the pillow.

"Now you're pushing it, mister." I reached under the comforter to tickle his foot. "I thought you might actually get up and make yourself presentable."

He grunted. "Or you could just bring me coffee in here."

"That would be rude to Mrs. Mac. She'd think you don't want to see her."

Lucas snorted and then twisted to look at me. "Hey, didn't I lock the back door last night? How'd she get in?"

"She has a key, and she's not shy about using it." I shrugged. "Sorry. I've tried to discourage it, but she always has an excuse I can't argue with. Like what if I were trapped under a heavy piece of furniture? Or if I'd had a stroke and needed help?"

"Yeah, but that was before. Before me. Before *us*." He snagged my hand as I passed the bed, on my way to bathroom. "I think you're covered now."

"True, but I don't want to hurt her feelings. So I'll go out there and see what's going on, and then you can come out and put in an appearance." I bent to kiss his forehead. "Because you don't want to hurt her feelings either."

Lucas made a noise that was a mix of a sigh and a moan, but he let go of my hand. I dug a pair of yoga pants out of my drawer and pulled them on under my big T-shirt. No bra, but hey, Mrs. Mac had let herself into my house before nine o'clock. She had to take what she got.

"Good morning!" She sang out the words as I came into the kitchen. "I started coffee. And I brought sticky buns."

I nearly tripped over my own feet. "You brought breakfast? Really? Wait, am I dying? What do you know that I don't?"

"Oh, you silly girl." Mrs. Mac chuckled and poured me a mug of coffee. "I just thought you and your young man might like a treat."

"Hmmmm." I eyed her over the rim of my cup. I couldn't help being suspicious. This was behavior entirely unlike my favorite neighbor—wait, make that my favorite *female* neighbor—unless, of course she wanted something, and I couldn't think what that might . . .

"Oh!" I set down my coffee on the table with a thunk. "This is about information, isn't it? Somehow you found out—" I broke off. If I was wrong and she didn't know yet that Lucas had been on the scene of Maddy's death, I didn't want to let the cat out of the bag.

But the older woman's face clearly showed her guilt. "Norma heard from Poor Myrtle who'd talked to Emily Shunt. You know her grandson's on the police force down here."

I shook my head. "So much for closed-mouth cops. What exactly did you hear?"

"Not too much. Just that Lucas was there, in Maddy's office. What was he doing there?"

I wracked my brain to remember his cover story. "Uh, well, it turned out he knew her, slightly, years ago, and he heard she was in the area, so he just stopped by." I wondered if the mojo that kept Lucas from being implicated in a death extended to the agile mind of Mrs. Mac. Apparently the answer was yes, because she didn't persist in questioning me as I'd have expected. "I thought Emily Shunt was still up north for her niece's wedding. How did Poor Myrtle talk to her?"

"Poor Myrtle called her. She wanted to get the skinny on how Maddy died, because she owns the office building, and the police wouldn't let her go in. Emily told her she should talk to Lucas, because he was there."

I sipped my coffee and raised one eyebrow. "So why isn't Poor Myrtle here with sticky buns? How did you get the job?"

"Well, I'm right next door, and Poor Myrtle pointed out that maybe you'd be more open to talking with me." She patted the white paper box on the table. "And she supplied the bakery goods."

"Aha. I knew you'd never bring breakfast on your own." I sat back in my chair. "So what do you and your cronies need to know?"

"Poor Myrtle needs to know about the bodily-fluids situation." Mrs. Mac nodded sagely. "So she can figure out if she'll need to have the carpets replaced before she lists it again."

Poor Myrtle was our local real estate agent and magnate. Many, many years before, when she was only eighteen, she'd gotten married on a whim. When her groom took off after a month of wedded bliss, Myrtle signed up for a course in real estate, earned her license and subsequently established a multi-million-dollar business. She'd sold it when she moved down here, but boredom had prompted her to open a smaller real-estate agency in Palm Dunes. And although clearly Poor Myrtle was anything but, all the women in Golden Rays continued to refer to her thus, simply because she'd never remarried.

"Can't she just wait until the police clear her to go back in? I wouldn't think it'd be long."

"You know Poor Myrtle. She likes to get a jump on these things." Mrs. Mac narrowed her eyes at me. "And we all think it's a little odd that the cops sealed the scene. Everyone's saying she died, but no one says how."

"Hmmm." I was noncommittal. "What's the top theory among Palm Dunes' amateur force?"

"Drug dealer. You know these music types. They're all involved in drugs. And they get their clients hooked on them. Look at Elvis."

I choked on my coffee. "Um, Mrs. Mack, don't you think it's a little bit of a leap from Maddy Cane, who's a small-time manager for a folk singer, to the King of Rock n' Roll?"

She blinked. "I don't know what you mean."

Luckily for me, Lucas chose that moment to stroll into the kitchen. "Good morning, ladies. Is that coffee I smell?"

Mrs. Mac jumped to her feet. "It is! And look. I brought you sticky buns, too. From Lurlene's."

"Wow." Lucas opened the silverware drawer and took out a knife. "And Jackie said it was doubtful you'd bring breakfast." He shook his head and tsk'd, looking at me sadly. I saw the gleam of humor in his eyes. He totally knew the score. He'd probably been standing just outside, listening to Mrs. Mac talk to me.

Mrs. Mac chose to ignore what he'd said. "Lurlene's is the best." She took the knife from Lucas and cut the string on the box then pushed back her chair. "Here, you sit down and let me get you a plate."

Lucas did as she said, waiting while Mrs. Mac bustled around, pouring his coffee and cutting the buns. When she unfolded a napkin and draped it over his lap, I couldn't help rolling my eyes.

"Oh, for crying out loud. She wants information, and she's bribing you with breakfast."

"Jackie." Mrs. Mac managed to look both shocked and disappointed. "Now that's just not true. Maybe I wanted to do something neighborly."

"Uh huh. And maybe pigs are flying now."

"What did you want to know, Mrs. Mac?"

She shot me a triumphant look. "We—that is, Poor Myrtle and I wanted to know about the office where Crissy's manager died. Was it torn up? Any damage to the walls or the carpet? Did it look like there'd been a struggle? And what do the police think happened? Was it a hit man?"

To his credit, Lucas didn't show any surprise. His lips didn't so much as twitch as he pretended to consider Mrs. Mac's words.

"You know, I promised I wouldn't say anything. The police asked me not to. But I think I can tell you this much." He lowered his voice and leaned forward. "No damage to any part of the office. Poor Myrtle should be able to turn it over pretty fast as soon as it's cleared by the cops."

Mrs. Mac's face fell. "No blood stains? No bullet holes?"

"Not even one. Sorry."

"Then what happened? How did she die? Was it just a heart attack or something?" The idea of plain old cardiac arrest clearly didn't sit well with Mrs. Mac's sense of drama.

"Can't say."

She crossed her arms over her chest and scowled. "So I hauled my cookies—and these sticky buns—over here at the crack of dawn for nothing?"

I pasted on a sweet smile. "You found out what Poor Myrtle needed to know, Mrs. Mac. Mission accomplished."

"Hmph." She raised one eyebrow at me. "He told *you*, didn't he?"

"Telling me isn't like telling the Golden Rays hotline. I know how to keep my mouth shut."

She reached for the bakery box, and snapping down the lid, picked it up. "I'm taking my sticky buns home to share with others who can't keep their mouths shut."

I laughed. "Thank you for bringing over breakfast, Mrs. Mac! We love you."

"Yeah, yeah, yeah." She slammed the door behind her, grumbling all the way.

"That seals the deal, you know." I grinned at Lucas. "Today, you're going to be the most popular guy in Golden Rays. And that's saying something, since Mr. Beck got his hair transplant last week. Get ready."

Lucas stood up and stretched. "Aw, you're just jealous because you didn't get any sticky buns. And I'm sure you're exaggerating. This isn't going to be that big a deal."

By late afternoon, Lucas was eating his words. Well, he would've been eating them, if he hadn't been too busy eating cookies, brownies, fudge, chicken pot pie and a variety of other foods that arrived at his house in the hands of women who were sure they'd be the ones to break his self-imposed silence.

I was glad he'd gone home after breakfast; the parade of the morbidly-curious skipped my house and beat a path to his front door. I had a front-row seat as I worked on my latest incarnation of pecan pie, this time with a ribbon of caramel running through the nuts. It was delicious, but I still wasn't sure it was *the* pie. I was certain that in order to beat Bitsy, the winning pie would have to be outstanding from the first bite. It would have to leave the taster weak in the knees, sagging in her chair as she fanned herself before devouring the rest of the slice. I wasn't there yet.

When there was a lull in the visits, Lucas jogged across the grass that linked our houses. He opened the back door and stuck his head into the kitchen.

"Hey, how about we eat at my house tonight? I seem to have a lot of food."

I raised my eyebrows, feigning ignorance. "Oh, really? How did that happen?"

"Okay, just stop. I know you've been watching all the females of Golden Rays stream into my house. I give. You were right. They all wanted to pump me for details about Maddy." He lowered his voice, as though someone might overhear us. "Some of them were downright creepy about it."

"Creepy in that they wanted the gory details, or creepy in that they were offering you a little something-something—and I *don't* mean meatloaf—in exchange for said info?"

"First, eww. Definitely the former. None of them made any moves on me."

"That you picked up on, anyway. Sometimes men can be a little dense when it comes to women coming onto them."

"Somehow I think you're talking about more than the old ladies here, but I'm not going there. Will you come over to eat?"

"Of course. Always happy to help when it comes to food. Makani!" I called, and my sweet pup came out from under the table, doing a long and luxurious full-body stretch. He wagged his tail at Lucas and then trotted after us as we walked across the lawn, stopping to lift his leg on his favorite bush.

Lucas wasn't kidding about the bounty of food. I must've missed a few women, I decided, as we served up full plates. "We should freeze some of this. We'll never eat it all today. Or maybe even this week."

"Sounds like a good plan. Or we could have a party. Invite a bunch of people over, serve some wine and beer, let them eat."

"Uh huh. And just who would you invite? Most of our friends are the ones who brought you the food you're trying to get rid of. Oh, and Nichelle. We could invite her family over. I've seen them eat, and they'd make short work of this."

"Hmm." Lucas scooped a spoonful of mashed potatoes into his mouth.

"I don't know why you two don't like each other. You're both lovely people. You must be, because I like you both."

"Nicelle doesn't like me?" He frowned. "Why not?"

I shrugged. "I have no idea. And I don't know that she doesn't like you, but I'm not sure she trusts you. Can you blame her? She delivers blood to your house every three days. Speaking of which, aren't you about due for a delivery?"

"Tomorrow. Which is good, because I'm out."

My stomach tightened. I wasn't squeamish so much anymore about the fact that my boyfriend drank blood, but neither did I enjoy sitting around watching him do it. But it was more the idea that his need for blood seemed to be increasing that made me nervous. It made me wonder if his supernatural side was growing. I remembered the night—or more accurately, the early morning—before we'd performed the ritual that had led to my possession. Lucas had drunk from me, as he almost always did when we made love. But it had been different. In the gray light before dawn, he'd seemed almost unable to stop. He'd pulled himself away, yes—but with more difficulty than ever before. Since that was the last time we'd been together, it stuck in my mind, and my unease grew.

"Hey, you still with me?" Lucas leaned across the coffee table, where we were eating, and kissed me lightly. "You disappeared for a minute."

I forced a smile. "Yeah, I'm fine. Just thinking."

"Well, don't. Or if you're going to, give me a head's up. It freaks me out when you go blank. When Delia—" He shook his head. "It was fucking horrible, looking into your eyes and not seeing *you* looking back. I never want that to happen again."

"I'm on board with that. And I—" The doorbell rang, and I jumped as Makani stood up and barked. "Who—oh, crap, is that more food? I thought everyone would be home getting ready for bed by now."

Lucas set his plate on the table and stood, moving toward the front door, the pup at his heels. He glanced through the side window and then opened the door. I couldn't see beyond him to who was there, even when I craned my neck. But I could hear their voices.

"Hey." Lucas sounded surprised. "How—I mean, what

can I do for you?"

"I'm sorry. I should've called, I guess." No, that wasn't the voice of an older woman. I knew who it was, and my heart pounded.

"No, no. It's fine. Come on in." Lucas stood back, and Crissy Darwin walked through his front door.

"Oh, I'm interrupting." She spotted me and stopped, clutching her hands together.

"Not at all. Crissy, this is my girlfriend, Jackie O'Brien. Jackie, you know Crissy Darwin."

"Yes." With carefully controlled movements so I didn't do something stupid like leap to my feet and squeal like a teen-aged groupie, I set my plate down and stood. "I mean, I know of her. Of you. Nice to meet you."

"Hey, I know you, don't I? I've seen you at shows, I think."

"Yes." It seemed to be the one safe word to say. "Yes. I've been at all your local performances."

"Well, thanks. It's always so great to meet someone who's been following me from the get-go." She bent to rub her knuckles on Makani's furry white head as he begged for attention.

I hadn't seen Crissy in nearly a year, since most of her gigs had taken her outside the state or in parts of Florida far from Palm Dunes. She'd grown up, I realized; her face, always pretty in a cute and girlish way, had thinned out a little, giving her defined cheekbones and make her green eyes look even larger. Blonde hair was secured in a single braid down her back, and she was dressed casually in jeans and a black scoop-necked shirt. Her voice was soft, giving no indication of the range and power it displayed on the stage.

"Won't you sit down?" Lucas pointed to the winged arm chair adjacent to the sofa.

"But you're eating. I don't want to disturb you."

"Nah, we're just . . ." He spread his hands over the food. "A bunch of neighbors brought over food today, and we're trying to eat as much of it as possible. Can I bring you a plate?"

"Thanks, but I ate with my parents." She perched on the edge of the chair, and Lucas came around the table to sit next to me. "I know this is weird. But I needed to—you found Maddy. I just needed to talk to someone else who was there. I'm freaking out. I keep seeing her—the way her eyes were staring, and her mouth, and her body, the way it was twisted—"

"Crissy." Lucas leaned forward to cover her hands with one of his. "You've got to stop thinking about it. Try to remember Maddy from before. The way she looked when she laughed, or when she was talking to you. Don't let yourself go down that path. It'll eat you up."

"I can't help it. Every time I close my eyes, that's what I see. I had to take a sleeping pill last night. I stayed at my parents' house—I just got my own apartment last month, and here I am back in my old bedroom. It's killing me. I don't understand what happened, and why."

"Have the police told you anything? I mean, you don't have to tell me," Lucas hastened to add. "But I just wondered if you had more information."

"Not anything specific, except that the ME is fairly certain it was poison. They'll tell me more tomorrow, I guess. But one thing they didn't have to tell me." She hunched her shoulders.

"I saw what Maddy had been eating. It was on her desk. It was Kung Pao shrimp. That's got to be where the poison came from."

"Okay." Lucas nodded. "If it was a fast-acting poison, that makes sense."

"But you don't understand. The Kung Pao shrimp was mine. I was supposed to meet Maddy for lunch yesterday at her office, and I told her I'd order food for us and have it delivered. I did it online, and they ask you to assign names to each dish. You know? So I ordered Kung Pao shrimp for me, with my name, and then I ordered her Hunan shrimp. But the box that was opened on her desk—that was Kung Pao. I always used to tease her about not being able to figure out which was which. If I didn't specifically show her, she always ended up thinking mine was hers."

Lucas frowned. "So let me get this straight. When she died, Maddy was eating food that was intended for you? You're sure?"

"Positive. I saw the peppers. I watch out for them, because if you eat them, they burn really bad."

I glanced from Lucas to Crissy. "So you think someone was trying to poison you, and Maddy ate the food by mistake?"

"I don't know what to think." Crissy covered her face. "I can't think why anyone would want to do it. The police told me it was probably a random thing, some crazy person wanting to lash out at someone he didn't know. But even so, it was supposed to be me, not Maddy. She made a mistake, and it killed her."

"You told the cops about this? About the shrimp being

your meal?" Lucas rubbed his jaw.

Crissy nodded. "I did. Right away. I don't think they saw how it was important."

"If it's what they think, then it probably isn't." Lucas kept his words gentle. "I know it feels like you could've done something, but you couldn't. It was just one of those things."

"If I'd been on time to lunch though . . . . I was always late. If I'd picked up the food instead of having it delivered, I would've made sure she had the right meal."

"And you'd be dead instead of Maddy." Lucas patted her hands. "Do you think she'd have wanted that?"

"Of course not." She sniffled. "I know she wouldn't. I guess you're right, it was just random. An accident." Fumbling in her pocket, she pulled out a tissue and dabbed at her nose. "Thank you. I needed to talk about it, and my mom and dad won't let me. They keep telling me to put it out of my mind. I think they're afraid I'm going to mess up this chance for the contract. Go off the deep end and not be able to perform."

"I'm sure they're worried about you, and they don't want you to lose any opportunity." I spoke up at last. "You're amazingly talented. If Maddy was as passionate about your career as you and your parents are, she wouldn't want this to derail it."

"I guess. That's what my father says, too."

"Do you have someone who can—" I began, but Lucas suddenly jumped to his feet and caught my eye.

"Uh, Jackie, cantaloupe."

Realization swept over me. "Okay, I got this."

He turned and left the room, disappearing into the kitchen,

where in a matter of seconds, he would, in fact, disappear for real, transported to yet another death scene for a Reckoning. Months ago, when we'd first ventured into public as a couple, we'd come up with this safe word that alerted me when he felt a transportation coming on. It meant I had to cover for him while he high-tailed it to a men's room or a back alley or a different room in a house to vanish in relative privacy.

I turned to Crissy. "Sorry about that. Lucas has a—a condition, and sometimes he needs to be alone. He had to go lie down. It comes on him very suddenly." I smiled and tried to look like I wasn't rattled at being left alone abruptly with a distraught young woman who happened to be someone I fangirled over.

She stood up, too. "I'm sorry, again. I might've upset him, talking about Maddy, when I guess they were old friends?" She looked at me as though she expected me to have the answers.

"As I understand it. Maybe not so much friends as acquaintances. I don't know much, though. I think stopping in to see her yesterday was kind of an impulsive thing." I forced my lips to stretch further and prayed she didn't ask me for any details. "But I don't think you upset him. This—his, uh, situation—it doesn't have anything to do with being upset. Or you. It's just a . . . thing."

"Thanks for saying that. And you've both been very kind to me today. I'll get going now—my parents are waiting for me to come home. They're a little freaked, too, even though they try to hide it from me." She headed for the foyer, and I trailed her.

Just before she opened the door, Crissy paused with her

hand on the knob. "Will you be at the Pecan Festival? I think I remember you from there. And I know it's a big deal here in Palm Dunes." The corners of her lips turned up a little. "It's the first place I performed in public."

"I know, I was there." I blurted it out, and yeah, I sounded gushy. I tried to find some of my lost composure. "You were amazing."

"Thank you. I was scared shitless." She winked at me. "I hope I've improved since then."

"If you need any help, anything at all, I'd be happy to be there for you. I'm going to be at the Triple P, entering my pecan pie in the contest. At least, I hope I am. I haven't found the right recipe yet."

Now her smile was genuine. "Oh, my favorite entry always came from Leone's! I loved Al. He used to make sure I got a big old slice delivered to me backstage." Her eyes dimmed a little. "And now he's gone, too."

"I actually bought Leone's from Al's family. I had no idea Al did that for you, with the pie. He never mentioned it."

"He was a sweet man. I'm going to miss him this year."

A thought occurred to me. "Hey, did you know that before he died, Al and I put together a cookbook of his favorite recipes? I have a copy of it at my house, if you'd like one. It's just next door."

Her face lit up. "Oh, definitely! Thanks. Will you sign it for me?"

"Sure. Just let me run over and grab it." I hesitated, remembering that Lucas had no control of which room in the house he'd re-appear in when the Reckoning was over. It would really send poor Crissy over the edge if Lucas popped back into the living room while she stood there waiting for me. "On second thought, why don't you just walk over with me?"

We made our way through the dimming light, with Makani wandering between us. Crissy elected to wait on the front porch petting the dog while I dashed inside and found one of the glossy hardback books. Seeing the cookbook always made me a little sad; Al had been so excited about it. Making it real had helped get me through my initial grief after he'd been killed; my editors at *Food, International* had been more than happy to publish it, and the small royalty payments I'd received—Al's family rightfully got most of it—had helped me make the transition after I'd left my columnist job. It was my last link to a man who'd been a dear friend and surrogate grandfather.

I handed the book to Crissy. "Everything in here is his. We were able to go over all the recipes before he died." I sighed. "I only wish I'd thought to convince him to hand over his pecan pie recipe. My entry is going to represent Leone's this year, and I'm worried I won't be able to do it justice."

"I'm sure you will." Crissy opened the book and smiled at Al's face on the title page. "You'll make it your own, right? So you'll have just as much chance as Al always did. And he'd be proud of you for keeping up the tradition." She lifted the book. "Thank you for this. It means a lot."

"You're very welcome. I guess I'll see you next week at the Festival?"

"Absolutely." She leaned forward and gave me a quick hug. "I'll dedicate a song to you."

I walked Crissy to her car and waved as she pulled away.

Picking up Makani, I made my way back to Lucas's house, lost in thoughts of Al, Maddy, poisoned Kung Pao shrimp and perfect pecan pie.

Chapter 5

I WAS SUFFOCATING. I couldn't breathe, couldn't scream, couldn't beg for help or mercy. Paralyzed, I could almost feel my heartbeat slowing, its rhythm at odds with the panic clutching at me. I was trying to hold on, trying not to be pushed into oblivion, but then there was nothing, only darkness, and nothing to grasp. Awareness dimmed to nothing . . . until it came roaring back, accompanied by the most horrendous, heart-breaking scream I'd ever heard. She cried piteously as she pleaded not to be sent back, not to be forced to the gray place. And then there was a most exquisite pain, as though a huge scab was being ripped from a wound I didn't know I had. I curled against the hurt, struggling to hold on when—

"Jackie! Wake up. Come on, honey. Babe, open your eyes. You're all right. You're here, you're with me. You're safe. No one's going to hurt you. Jackie, baby, look at me."

My eyelids fluttered, and I saw Lucas leaning over me, his eyes filled with worry and anguish. It brought me back to his expression that afternoon after Delia, and for a moment, I was afraid I was there again, somehow taken away in time.

But no. I was in my own bed, back in Palm Dunes, and Lucas was with me. I let him draw me against him, the skin on his bare chest warm where my cheek rested against it. He stroked my hair and murmured words I couldn't understand until my breathing had nearly returned to normal.

"Are you okay?" His words were muffled against my hair.

"Yeah." I burrowed my face deeper into his neck. "Just a dream. A nightmare."

"Baby, was it Delia? Was that what you were dreaming about? The possession?"

I briefly considered lying, but I was too shaken to do it. "Yeah. It was like it was happening again. Like I was back there. And I couldn't—I couldn't get away. I thought I was lost."

"You'll never be lost, Jackie. I promise you. I'd never let you be. I'd follow you down the darkest path, and I'd risk anything to bring you back." He kissed my forehead and then each cheek. "I own your soul, baby. And I'll never let you go."

Tears wet my face, but I wasn't sure if they were left over from my dream or springing from the words Lucas spoke. I closed my eyes again and plastered my body as close to him as I could get.

"Hold me?" It was all I could manage.

"Forever. And then some." He wrapped his arms tighter around me, and after a few minutes, I slid into a dreamless sleep.

I slept later the next morning than I had in a long time, waking up only when Lucas brought me a tray of coffee and muffins he'd gotten from Lurlene's. I pushed to sit up.

"Wow. So is this a bribe for information, like Mrs. Mac?"

"Ha." He settled the tray and sat down next to me, snagging a muffin. "No." He took a huge bite and then cocked his head, watching me as he swallowed. "Or then again, maybe it is." He brushed back the hair from my face. "I want to talk with you about last night."

I stiffened and stared into my coffee mug. "It was just a nightmare."

"Yes, it was. I get that. But it was more than that, too. If you're still having such disturbing dreams, I don't think you've dealt with this yet. I know you don't want to talk about it, but maybe you need to."

I brushed the crumbs from my muffin into a tiny pile. "I don't want to talk to Zoe. I know you like her, and I guess she's okay, but I don't want her picking through my brain."

"Okay. But I don't think a regular counselor's going to work, either. When you explain you were possessed, you may find yourself in the nearest mental hospital."

"No, I know." I lifted my shoulder. "I'll think about it, okay? Will that do for now? I promise. I'm not going to sweep this under the rug."

Lucas studied me for a few seconds, staring into my eyes until I dropped my gaze. "Okay. If you promise." He tipped up my chin with two of his fingers. "Hey. You know I'm just worried, right? And I want you to be . . . peaceful. I don't want this to torment you."

I nodded. "I know."

"I love you, Jacks."

I nodded again. "I know that, too."

I moved through the rest of my day in a haze, feeling slightly drugged and slightly hung over at the same time. I worked half-heartedly on another pecan pie recipe—this time, with the addition of walnuts and maple syrup. Lucas, being the unselfish giving type, tried a piece and pronounced it delicious.

"But is it the best pecan pie you've ever had?" I stood across from him, my hands folded over my chest.

He hesitated, and I nodded. "Yep. See, I'm glad you like it, but if it doesn't absolutely blow your mind, I can't enter it in the contest. I need to know I have a reasonable chance of beating Bitsy."

Lucas finished his last bite of crust. "I get it." His forehead drew together, and he shook his head. "No, I guess I don't. You've been working so hard to come up some spectacular pecan pie recipe, but why? Is it the end of the world if this Bitsy wins one year?"

I snorted. "Clearly you forget that the end of the world is starting with that old guy in the nursing home on the West Coast. And no, of course it wouldn't be. But I want to win. I want to win for Al, for everyone at Leone's and for me. It's like a way to remember Al, to pay tribute to him, you know? Like a tip of the hat. A twenty-one-gun salute. It's something I need to do."

He grinned. "All right then. As long as you're clear on the whys, I'm more than happy to support this worthy cause."

"Good." I patted his cheek. "Because I need to run to the grocery store for more supplies, and it would be super if you'd walk Makani and give him dinner while I'm gone."

Lucas sighed. "Of course. You know what they say. A man's work is never done."

I rolled my eyes. "Dude, that is so wrong, I'm not even going to acknowledge it. I'll be back in about half an hour. We'll heat up some of that chicken pot pie from Mrs. Gent." Grabbing my keys from the hook by the door, I sent both my boys an airy wave as I left fast, before they could change their minds about letting me go.

I'd said I was going to the grocery store, but my first stop was actually the farmers' market, which this month was bringing in an extra-large supply of pecans from Georgia in preparation for the Festival. I invested in a few pounds, chatted with the woman who ran the stand, and then headed for my favorite Palm Dunes food market.

Hardy Brothers was not the closest store to Golden Rays, so when I needed something quick, like milk or bread, I tended to run to the Shop and Save on the corner, just outside the community. But Hardy Brothers was a store with history, established in the late 1950's, before Golden Rays was even conceived. The store stocked plenty of local favorites, along with some specialty items from the Northeast that I could only get there. I loved it, since it felt like a little piece of home down here in the Sunshine State.

Today I wasn't at Hardy Brothers looking for any particular item; instead, I was searching for inspiration. I'd run out of variations of pecan pie, and my mind, a little numb from my interrupted sleep, needed some help.

Pushing the basket—or the buggy, as the locals referred to it—I wandered the aisles, stopping now and then to examine one thing or another.

"Why, if it isn't the runner up to the Perfect Pecan Pie Festival! Jackie O'Brien, as I live and breathe."

I closed my eyes and gritted my teeth. Of all the people in all the world, what was the chance that I'd run into Bitsy Ray at Hardy Brothers?

"Hello, Bitsy." I turned, pasting a huge phony smile on my face. "I wasn't aware the judging for the pie contest had happened yet." I leaned toward her, lowering my voice. "Have you been indulging a little early, honey? Tippling some of the cooking wine?"

Her plump face went red. "You're the one who's going to want to get drunk at the Festival, when I walk away with the ribbon that's rightfully mine. All those years of Al Leone rubbing it in my face . . . well, those days are over. This year, it's mine. This is Bitsy's year!"

More than a few people had stopped to gawk as Bitsy's voice got shriller and louder. I saw a couple exchange significant looks.

"Bitsy, Al never rubbed it in your face. He was the kindest man who ever lived, and he would've done anything for any of us. He tried to help you when you started up your business. He wanted to be a friend. But you threw it back at him every single time. I can't imagine anyone would've been as gracious as Al was for as long as he was."

Something passed through Bitsy's eyes. I wasn't sure what it meant, but I would've sworn I saw a flash of regret before the hatefulness took over again. "Think what you will. Think whatever makes you feel better. Because next week, when they're announcing winners, you can bet your sweet ass it's going to be my name winning first prize."

With a grand sweep of her head, Bitsy stomped down the aisle, toward the check-out counter. I sighed, rubbing my temples and wishing I could transport like Lucas did. Only not to death scenes. I'd just transport home.

"Well, that woman seems a trifle unhappy, doesn't she?"

I turned to find a diminutive older lady standing with her hand on her buggy, watching me with raised eyebrows.

"I'm sorry." I wasn't sure why it was *me* apologizing for

Bitsy's bad manners, but somehow I was. "I guess she's just very passionate about, uh, pecans."

"Oh, honey!" The woman waved her hand at me, laughing. "Honey, I grew up in a family of people *consumed* by pecans. We ate them, we slept them, we talked about them *ad naseum* . . . and I can tell you for sure and certain, none of us ever behaved like that." She dropped her honeyed voice to just above a whisper. "She was not acting like a lady at all. I don't like that."

I smiled, anger seeping away a bit. "I don't blame you. But I should've just walked away, I guess."

"Oh, no, you were just standing up for yourself. And for your friend. You knew Al Leone, did you? Now *there* was a gentleman. He knew how to make a lady feel special, didn't he?"

"He did." My eyes blurred with tears. Bitsy's nastiness had upset me more than I'd realized. "He was a special man."

"Yes, he was. Have you been by Leone's since he passed? I heard the new owner's kept it very much the same. I've dragged my feet over going back, just because I dread seeing the place without Al there to greet me."

I wanted to hug this lady. "I'm actually the new owner, and I'm glad you've heard that. We've worked hard to keep it exactly as Al would like. I hope you'll come back, and soon. I'll make sure you're our guest of honor."

"Oh, honey, aren't you sweet." She paused, scrutinizing me up and down. "Are you entering a pie in the Festival this year? Is that what that wretched woman was going on about?"

"It was. And yes, I am. Bitsy thinks it's her turn to win,

though. That's why she's, uh, so wretched."

"Well, that's a real shame. Because this kind of nastiness is not what the General intended when he created the Festival." Her lips curved into a smile and her light blue eyes twinkled. "I should know. The General was my grandfather."

"No!" I couldn't believe it. I'd heard rumors that General Casey still had some family around here, but I'd never actually met any of them. "But you . . . how can you be . . . wasn't General Casey in the Civil War?"

"The General did serve in the War of Northern Aggression, yes." She inclined her head. "And you're very kind, my dear, but I assure you, I'm quite old enough to be his granddaughter. Although I'll admit, both the General and Colonel—the Colonel was my father, you understand—both of them married rather late in life. The General was ninety when I was born. I don't remember a great deal about him, but I do know that he loved his pecans and he loved Palm Dunes. He used to tell us he wanted it to be the best of Florida and the best of Georgia, combined in one perfect community. That's why he called his Festival the Perfect Pecan Pie."

"That's such a sweet story, it really does capture the . . ." My voice trailed off as an idea took hold and unfolded in brilliant clarity. "Oh! Oh, Mrs. . . . dang, I don't know your name, I'm sorry. But you've given me a wonderful idea!"

"It's Belinda Casey Colby." She offered me her hand, and I shook it gently. "And I don't know quite what I said, but if I helped, I'm glad."

"I'm very happy to meet you, Mrs. Colby. I'm Jackie O'Brien. And trust me, what you just said made all the difference in the world. Now if you'll excuse me, I need to make a quick trip to the produce section."

Chapter 6

"SERIOUSLY. YOU'RE NOT going to tell me about the recipe you came up with? The one that's going to win you the blue ribbon?"

"I'm seriously not. It's a little daring, a little risky, and I don't need any naysaying. This kitchen is a no-negativity zone." I spread my arms wide. "Finish your oatmeal and then hit the road. Go to your house and work on those edits you've been putting off all week."

Lucas heaved a sigh. "Fine. Oh, hey, before I forget, though—Crissy texted me and invited us to come hear her tonight. It's her first time performing since Maddy died."

"Was murdered, you mean."

"Yes, Jackie, thanks for keeping me straight on that. I might've forgotten that important fact." He waited a beat, as though to see whether I'd respond to his sarcasm, and when I didn't, he went on. "Anyway, Crissy's singing tonight at some beach bar a little up the coast. What do you think? Want to go?"

I considered. "Actually, I'd love to go. I'm pretty sure this recipe is going to be the one, and if it is, I'll be in the mood to celebrate."

"Great. I'll let her know."

I stood up and began to clear the table. "So now Crissy Darwin's texting you? Is this something I should be worried about? I know your track record with younger women."

Lucas rolled his eyes. "No, you should not be worried. First of all, I don't see her that way. She's a nice kid who happens to be involved in a terrible situation. Second, she doesn't see me that way, either. And she knows you're my girlfriend. She likes you."

"Has she heard anything else from the police, about Maddy?"

Lucas picked up his bowl and carried it to the sink. "I guess they confirmed that it was poison. Strychnine, cut with something else that sped up how fast it acted. They found the guy who delivered the food to the office building. He said usually, he calls up to whoever ordered the food and tells them he's in the lobby so they can come down to pay him and take the food, but this time, someone met him there, paid him and took the food up. Had the names and everything, so he thought it was cool."

"So do they think that's where the poisoning happened?"

"It's the only place in the whole process where it could've happened, assuming it wasn't someone at the restaurant or the delivery guy, and both of those seem unlikely. Crissy said they're having the delivery guy work with a police artist, and they'll release the sketch tomorrow."

"The cat'll be out of the bag about it being murder, then."

"It will. Which is another reason I thought it'd be good for us to be at her performance tonight."

"I'm on board. I can't wait for you to hear her sing."

Lucas nodded, but his eyes were focused somewhere over my shoulder. "How long is it going to take you to make this pie? I was thinking maybe we'd go down a little early, walk on the beach. Eat dinner before Crissy goes on."

"The beach is always a good plan. I'll be done by lunch time, I think, unless I've really messed up the measures. Should we say early afternoon?"

"I'll be ready by then. Guess I'll tackle these edits, as someone so subtly suggested." He kissed me and tweaked my nose. "I'll see you in a bit."

By the time Lucas came to the door, calling to me, I was dressed and waiting. We let Makani out for a quick turn around the yard, then locked the door behind us as we left.

"Okay, so tell me. How did this recipe turn out? Was it everything you hoped?"

I grinned. "And then some. It's perfect. I think it's going to have a real good shot at beating Bitsy."

"Congratulations. Is that a weight off your mind?"

"It really is. And you know, between talking to Crissy and Mrs. Colby about Al, I feel like he was a part of this whole process. I know it sounds weird, but it's almost like I found him again. Does that sound crazy?"

"Jacks, nothing sounds crazy to me anymore. I think that's great. I know how much you've been missing him."

We drove along the coast with the windows down, taking the beach road instead of the highway. It took a little longer, but we still arrived in Crystal Cove before four o'clock. It was my favorite kind of autumn beach weather: the sun was warm, but not hot, the breeze was cooling without being chilling, and the sand was practically empty.

After he parked the car, Lucas turned to me, an expression I couldn't quite read on his face. "So I have a surprise for you. I hope you'll like it."

Surprises were so *not* my favorite thing. I pinned him with a dark look. "Lucas, what've you done?"

"Hey, are you two going to sit in the car all day or get out and be sociable?"

I jerked in my seat, turning to look out the open window where Rafe Brooks stood, grinning down at me. I pushed open my door and hopped out.

"Rafe! What're you doing here?" I hugged him, and he wrapped his strong arms around me in a tight embrace. Rafe was nearly twenty years my junior, but outside Lucas and Al, I'd never been more comfortable with a guy. There wasn't anything icky about it; we connected on a deep level and had an inordinate amount of affection for each other. It helped that we shared a wicked sense of humor, an irreverence that drove his Carruthers boss, Cathryn Whitmore, absolutely crazy.

"Lucas called this morning and told us you guys were coming here." He reached back to draw his girlfriend Nell forward, slinging an arm over her shoulder. Nell Massler wasn't precisely beautiful; her coloring was startling, with her jet black hair and her vibrant blue eyes. Her skin was so pale as to be nearly translucent. At first glance, she and Rafe seemed to be an odd couple, but I knew they were deeply and passionately in love.

"And you two just happened to be in the neighborhood?"

Nell smiled. It was a rare occurrence that she did, and I lapsed into silence, realizing that actually she was extraordinarily lovely.

"We were here in September, and I liked the burgers." She glanced up to Rafe, and his arm tightened around her.

"That's true. Hey, what can I say? We missed you guys. After our big bonding experience, life seemed a little too quiet without you around."

I laughed. "I find that hard to believe. You're in the hub of things, figuring out everything that's going down with the Hive. Isn't that enough excitement?"

"You're not wrong. Things are happening fast and furious." His gaze flickered to Lucas. "It's going to get intense, buddy. I hope you're ready."

Lucas held his eyes. "I hope so, too." He shifted to smile at Nell. "Hey, why don't we go in and grab some seats? Rafe said you have a story to tell about when you were here before. Something about a haunted hotel?" He offered the younger woman his arm.

"What about us?" Hands on my hips, I tilted my head. "Aren't Rafe and I invited?"

"I thought we might go for a walk on the beach." Rafe gestured toward the surf with a jerk of his head. "It was a long drive over here. I'd like some exercise before we eat."

"Sounds like a good idea. We'll be waiting inside. Take your time." Lucas and Nell wandered away from us.

I scowled at my boyfriend's departing back. "What is this, an intervention?"

Rafe took my hand. "Kind of. But not so much what you think." He pulled me toward the steps that led down to the ocean. "Come on. Let's walk a little."

For the first five minutes, neither of us spoke. I slid off my shoes as we stepped onto the sand and dangled them between two fingers. Rafe toed off his sneakers and left them under the dune steps, rolling up his pants to keep them dry.

The water was cold, and I shivered as it washed over my feet. Rafe sighed as he looked out over the endless blue waves.

"Nothing like the beach to remind us of our own finiteness, huh? When faced with what looks like infinity, I mean."

"Uh huh." Whatever this was all about, I didn't plan to make it easy on him.

"Jackie, I'm not going to give you a bunch of psychological bullshit. That's Zoe deal, and Lucas says you don't want to talk to her anymore. Which is cool. I get it. I mean, I love Zoe now, but when I first met her, I hated what she did." He slowed and laughed a little. "Actually, the first time I met her was in New Orleans, and I didn't know she worked for Carruthers. We were on a battlefield, and . . . well, it doesn't matter now. But she wanted to dig into crap I didn't want to touch, and I found that fucking annoying."

I nodded. "Exactly. And there's only so much you can say. I told her everything, and then what was left? She couldn't change how it felt. She couldn't go back in time and change what happened to me. She can't make me forget what it felt like when Delia pushed me down deep into my own mind, until I thought I was dead. And she can't make me un-hear Delia's screams as Lucas pulled her out of me and sent her . . . back."

"But I can." Rafe stopped and gripped my upper arms. "Jackie, how much do you know about what I can do?"

I scrunched up my forehead. "You're a manipulator. You can influence people's thoughts and perceptions, right? Kind of make them do things they might not otherwise do?"

"Yeah, that's right. I influence. It's not easy to convince people to do something huge that's against their will. It's much easier to manipulate emotions. Push on desires they already have."

"I can understand that."

"But I can also influence the perception of time. And I can make people forget things."

For a few beats, I was confused, and then understanding dawned. "You're offering to make me forget what happened with Delia?"

Rafe shrugged. "I'm just saying it's option." His mouth twisted into a parody of a smile. "I almost did it that day. Before you came around. I thought, I could easily make you forget everything. Save you a lot of pain and angst."

"Why didn't you?" I whispered.

He looked down at me, his green eyes full of understanding. "Because I feel pretty strongly that if it's possible, people should be free to decide what they remember and what they don't."

"Have you ever done it? Changed memories without people knowing it?"

Rafe's face shuttered. "I have. A few times. Once when a friend asked me to do it, out of compassion for someone we knew. Another time . . . when that same friend had become very important to me, and then she broke my heart. We were still in high school, and I couldn't stand our classmates whispering, talking about it . . . so I wiped their memories."

"What about hers? Did you wipe hers, too?"

He shook his head. "No. I wanted Tasmyn to remember me. To remember *us*. It was important to me at the time."

Tasmyn. The name rang a bell in my head, but I pushed that aside for now. "Any other times?"

He laughed, but there wasn't any real mirth. "Just about every night for four months, the summer after high school graduation. You remember when Nell told you I was a manwhore? She wasn't wrong. I slept my way through more cities than I care to admit. And every time I did, I wiped the woman's memory."

The thought of that made me reel. "All those women? How could you do that?"

His mouth tightened. "I did what I thought I needed to do. And I probably would've kept right on doing it, if I hadn't met a woman who called me on my shit. She knew me, had studied up on me, and when I slept with her and tried to erase her memory, she blocked me. That was a game-changer."

I blinked. "It was Joss, wasn't it?" I'd heard bits and pieces about the Carruthers agent who'd died saving Rafe's life on a Hive commune in Georgia, and then I'd met her when she'd returned as a ghost the same day I was possessed.

Life—and death—as a Carruthers agent—or even the girlfriend of a part-time agent—was complicated.

"Yeah, it was." His tone was carefully neutral.

"How's that going, by the way? Having Joss hanging around, I mean."

Rafe quirked one eyebrow. "Let's just say when Lucas asked if we wanted to come down here and meet you two, I didn't have to think about it. Don't get me wrong. Nell isn't jealous. And Joss is just as cool about stuff now that she's a, um, ghost as she was when she was alive. But still. It's a little wearing sometimes to have both my dead ex-girlfriend and my very-much-alive forever girlfriend both in the picture."

I giggled. "I can only imagine."

"But we're not here to talk about me. This is about you, Jackie. Do you want me to wipe your memory?"

I hesitated. "What would happen? What would I remember, and what would I forget?"

"I'm good at what I do, Jackie. You'd remember everything except the time when Delia was in control."

"Would it just be a blank?"

"No, you'd remember sitting on the sofa next to me."

I kicked at a wave that rolled over my toes. "Is there any risk? Like, that I might forget some really important stuff?"

Rafe shook his head. "No. I work like a neurosurgeon. Very precise." He paused. "The memories aren't exactly gone, Jackie. You just don't access them. But they can come back, under extreme circumstances. I wouldn't think it would be the case with you. But I need to say it."

I stooped to gather a handful of sand and let it sift through my fingers. "Would you do it? If you were me?"

He didn't miss a beat before answering. "No. I wouldn't choose to forget anything, not even the most painful stuff. And believe me, I've been tempted. But then, I'm not you, and I didn't go through what you did. I can't make the call for you."

I bit my lip. "Does Lucas think I should do it?"

Rafe patted my back. "You should probably ask him that, but honestly? I don't think he cares. He just wants you to have some peace. I don't think he cares how it happens."

For several minutes, I stood staring out over the ocean, thinking about what Rafe was offering me. I could forget Delia. I wouldn't have to hear her screams, hear her begging me not to make her leave. It would be over. I'd have peace.

But at what cost? Lucas would still remember that I'd been possessed. So would everyone else who'd been in that room, and when it came down to it, forgetting what had happened wouldn't change the fact that it had in fact taken place. Taking this path almost felt . . . cowardly. Like taking the easy way out. I hadn't asked to be possessed, but I was, and it had changed me.

"Do you think it's possible that things happen for a reason? What if something good was supposed to come out of this, and by forgetting it, I miss out? Or I miss something I'm supposed to do?"

"I do believe that. I believe in fate, and I believe in serendipity. I know that I went through hell, more than once, but it had to be that way for me to get here, now. And I wouldn't change the here and now for anything. Even as fucked-up as it is, with the world ending and all." He winked at me.

I squeezed his hand. "Thank you, Rafe. Thanks for being willing to help me, and coming down here to talk. I think I'm going to keep my memories. I just need to figure out a way to deal with them."

Rafe nodded. "How do you plan to do that? I'm willing to listen, if you think talking to me would help. Nell would be willing, too. She's not exactly the most compassionate person all the time, but I think she'd surprise you. She likes you, and Nell doesn't give her affection easily."

"I appreciate that. I don't know what will help me. I've tried thinking about it, not thinking about, pretending it never happened . . . but I can't stop hearing Delia. Rafe, I feel so damn guilty about sending her back. She was terrified. She pleaded with me not to make her go. But I did. I pushed her out, and then Lucas sent her back to the gray place."

"Jackie." Rafe's eyes were pained. "First of all, you had every right to push her out. She was occupying *your* body. You didn't invite her in or agree to let her visit. She forced her way in, possessed you and tried to keep you from coming back. You did what you had to do. Second, there's a reason Delia's in that gray place. I don't think she was evil, but she did some bad things. The only redeeming part of her was the part that loved Joss and took care of her."

I drew in a shaky breath. "I know all that logically. But it still feels wrong."

Rafe pulled me close into a friendly, comforting hug. I let him hold me for a minute before I pulled back.

"Jackie, I think I know where you need to start. Talk to Lucas. Tell him what you told me. Explain why you're struggling. Let him in. You won't begin to heal until you do that." He tugged on a lock of my hair. "And then maybe the two of you can get better together. That's the best way, you know?" He waggled his eyebrows at me. "Nell and I learned that. She says we both come with a ton of baggage, and if we don't let the other help carry it, we're both suffering. Let Lucas take a bag or two. I promise you, he can handle it."

I nodded. "Okay."

"Let's head back now. It's starting to get dark, and I'm a little worried about what trouble Lucas and Nell might get into if left to their own devices too long."

We strolled in peaceful silence. Just as we turned to head for the steps, I caught Rafe's hand. "How did you get to be so smart when you're still such a kid?"

He grinned. "Well, it wasn't clean living, baby."

Chapter 7

"THIS PLACE IS hopping!" I had to yell to be heard over the noise of the crowd gathering in the bar as Rafe and I joined Nell and Lucas.

Lucas slid his arm around my waist and pulled me against him, his eyes searching mine. I smiled and lifted my mouth to his, meeting his lips in a more open kiss than we'd shared in weeks.

"Thank you," I whispered into his ear.

He leaned back, his brows drawn together. "For what?"

"For loving me enough to offer me an out. Even if I didn't take it, I'm glad I had the option."

He traced one finger along my jaw. "Did it help? Talking

with Rafe, I mean?"

"I think so." I caught his hand and pressed my lips into the center of his palm. "We'll talk later. I promise."

"I'll hold you to that."

Our high-top table was covered with baskets of appetizers, and Rafe flagged down a passing waitress so we could order drinks.

"When does the music start?" He raised his voice to ask the question.

The server glanced at the clock above the bar. "Any time now. You fans? This girl is a big draw."

"She is." Lucas pointed at me. "The rest of us are hearing her for the first time."

"You'll love her." She picked up two empty baskets and whisked them away as she maneuvered between tables.

As if on cue, a shrill whistle cut through the noise, quieting conversations as all eyes turned to the small stage at one end of the restaurant. A pretty redhead stood in front of the microphone, waiting until she had the room's attention.

"Hey, y'all! Welcome to the Riptide! Tonight, we're excited to welcome back one of our favorites, rising star folk singer Crissy Darwin!"

The room erupted in shouts and applause as Crissy appeared, accompanied by a man carrying a guitar. She was flushed, smiling and glancing over the audience.

"Thank you, everyone, for coming out tonight! We're going to kick it off with one of my favorites and yours."

Without further ado, they launched into an upbeat number that had everyone clapping their hands and singing along.

The set moved along quickly, although I noticed Crissy didn't spend as much time as usual chatting between songs. I wondered how difficult it had been to take the stage tonight, with the sorrow over Maddy still so fresh and new.

After about forty-five minutes, Crissy paused at the microphone, gazing out over the audience. When she caught sight of Lucas and me, she smiled and gave us a slight nod.

"The next song is one of my new ones, and it's very close to my heart. I'd like to dedicate it to my friend and manager, Maddy Cane." She lifted her eyes up, kissed her fingers and raised them, as though throwing a kiss to heaven.

The ballad she sang was slow and heartbreaking, a song mourning lost love and missed chances. When the last note ended, I doubted there could be a dry eye in the house.

After that song, she took a break, bowing off and promising to return in twenty minutes for the second set. As the lights rose, I felt a tap on my shoulder.

"Are you Jackie?" The young woman behind me had glossy black hair and a huge brown eyes. "Hi, I'm Trina Wilson. Crissy sent me out to see if you and your friends would like to come back and say hello. She's got a private table out on the deck, and she'd love for you all to be her guests."

Rafe lifted his eyebrows. "Backstage passes? Guess it pays to know people who are connected."

As we rose to follow Trina, she turned back to beam a smile at us. "Crissy and I've been friends since grade school. She was so grateful to you for coming tonight. The last few days have been difficult."

"I can imagine." We filed out onto the deck, and the cool

night air made me shiver. Lucas wrapped his arm around me, tucking me close.

"Jackie, Lucas—thank you so much for coming." Crissy stood up from the table and met us both with a hug. "It was wonderful to see some friendly faces in the crowd."

"Are you kidding? This was great. And you had the crowd in the palm of your hand. They all love you."

"Thanks." A flicker of doubt crossed her face, but it vanished as she smiled at Rafe and Nell. "Hi, I'm Crissy. Thanks for coming."

We made the introductions all around, and then Crissy pointed to the man still sitting at the table. "That's Dell Jamison, my guitarist."

I smiled at the man who nodded at us. Beside me, Lucas twitched, but when I glanced up at him, he only shook his head slightly.

"And you met Trina, right? She's been helping me out for the last year, kind of my unofficial assistant."

"It's so much fun!" Trina gave Crissy a quick side-hug. "Crissy and I were in choir together for years, but she's the one who's making it big. I'm just happy to ride on her coattails."

The door from the restaurant opened, and the same waitress who was serving us came out, carrying a tray. "Here you go. Help yourselves, and if you need anything else, just let me know."

"Crissy!" The door flew open again, and this time a woman in a denim mini skirt and T-shirt rushed through, heading our way. Trina stood up, putting herself between Crissy and the newcomer. The woman slowed, raising her hands. "I know,

I know, this is your private time, but I just had to come back to say you totally killed it in the first set. The house was on fire." She squealed and clapped her hands.

"Thanks, Diane." Crissy sounded weary. "I appreciate it. You know I'm always grateful for your support."

"Oh, totally, you know you have that. My heart was just *breaking* for you tonight. Losing Maddy is a tragedy. I don't know how you even did it tonight, singing like everything was okay." She glanced at Lucas, Rafe, Nell and me, her eyes narrowing. "Oh, I'm sorry. You have company?"

"These are friends of mine, Diane. Diane's a super-fan." Crissy's voice was a tad brittle. "She comes to all my shows, no matter what."

"And I always will. I'm just dying here, waiting until I can download you into my iPod."

Trina took hold of Diane's arm, gently steering her away. "Crissy's got to eat now before she goes back on. Let's give her some privacy, okay?"

Diane shook off Trina's hand. "Oh, I know. I'm going." She waggled her fingers in a little wave. "See you all later. Bye, Dell. Bye, Crissy."

As she disappeared back into the restaurant, Crissy sighed. "I suppose I should be grateful. Diane follows me everywhere, re-posts all my stuff on social media and just *loves* everything I do."

"She's creepy." Trina made a face and picked up a bowl of chili. "And she makes me crazy, always pushing her way into things."

"She's just lonely." Dell spoke for the first time as he

reached for a hamburger. "Her life is empty, so she fills it up with someone else's stuff."

"God, Dell, that was deep." Crissy nudged him. "How many beers have you had?"

He shrugged. "Hey, I know Diane's weird. But I've talked to her before. She's harmless."

"Probably." Crissy turned back to us. "Let's talk about something else. You've met my crew here, but tell me how you all know each other."

Nell's eyes met mine, and I saw unfamiliar mirth there. Yeah, explaining how we'd met would definitely be complicated.

"I do some consulting work with the same company Rafe and Nell work for." Lucas reached for a French fry and dipped it into a small bowl of ketchup. Well, maybe it wasn't that complicated after all.

"That's cool. Oh, Jackie, my mom tried one of the recipes from Al's cookbook. Thanks again, so much. How's the search for the perfect pecan pie coming?"

"I think I've got it. I don't want to jinx anything, but this morning, I made what I hope will be this year's winner."

"I'm crossing my fingers for you." She smiled and then pulled out her phone to look at the time. "Crud, they're going to be calling me to go back on soon. Well, I'm glad we got to visit. I guess I'll see you at the Festival next week, right?" Crissy stood and twisted, stretching her back.

"Crissy, I don't feel so hot." Trina put her hand to her chest.

"Well, you scarfed up that chili pretty fast. No wonder

you have heartburn."

"I don't think it's heartburn. My stomach—" She clutched at her middle. "And my arms hurt." Trina pushed away from the table, but when she tried to stand, she listed to the side, her eyes rolling back in her head.

"Call 9-1-1!" Lucas shouted, and Rafe pulled out his phone. Vaguely I heard him muttering terse instructions.

Lucas and Dell lowered Trina to the deck floor, while Crissy dropped to her knees next to her friend. "Trina! Wake up. Come on, open your eyes." Her shoulders shook as she hovered over her friend.

Nell slipped away, going back into the bar. A few minutes later, she came back along with an older woman.

"She's a doctor," Nell murmured to me. "I thought it wouldn't hurt to have someone medical around until the paramedics arrive."

"Good thinking." I squeezed Nell's arm.

The doctor knelt by Trina, pulling open her eyes and asking us terse questions.

"You should know, this could be poisoning." Lucas spoke quietly. "Another associate of Crissy's was killed by strychnine earlier this week."

The doctor's eyes widened. "That tracks. Strychnine? Damn."

We heard sirens in the distance, growing louder as the ambulance came closer. Within seconds, the deck shook with the pounding of feet rushing over to us.

"Suspected poisoning. Get charcoal on board stat." Trina's body began to convulse, and the doctor cursed. "Dammit, she's seizing. We need phenobarbital. Miss, you need to move." She pushed Crissy out of the way.

The rest of us stood back, watching as the team worked on Trina. Faster than I expected, they had her on a stretcher, rolling her toward the steps that led to the street.

The doctor lingered, turning to us. "She's stable, and I think we probably acted fast enough. She's lucky. A little delay . . ." She shook her head. "You said someone else died of strychnine poisoning? What the hell are you people involved in?"

Crissy leaned into Dell as he held her close. He glanced at us.

"We don't know what's going on." Lucas's face was troubled. "But given two cases of poisoning around her, I think it's safe to say someone's trying to kill Crissy."

I'd known it, realized it must be the truth at some point as I'd watched them work on Trina. But hearing Lucas say it out loud made me go cold.

"What was she eating when she started getting sick?" The doctor looked at our table. "You'll need to have it tested. The police will want to bag all the evidence."

"They'll be here in a minute." Rafe lifted his phone. "I called them as soon as I heard what Lucas said about poisoning. Figured they'd want to get here while the scene was fresh."

"Good thinking." The doctor nodded.

As predicted, two uniformed policemen and one man in a suit who I presumed was a detective arrived within soon after. They questioned us all briefly and took the bowl of chili that Trina had been eating.

"Who ordered what?" The plainclothes detective looked around at us. "Was the chili specifically requested by Ms. Wilson?"

It was Crissy who answered, her voice shaky. "Usually we just order a bunch of food and share it. But Trina and I both love the chili here, so we always order two bowls of that. One with beans, for Trina, and one without, for me."

"And which bowl did she eat tonight?"

Crissy shrugged. "I honestly don't know. I didn't eat mine, because one of my fans came out right after the food was delivered. I ended up talking to her, and then after she went back inside, I just nibbled on some fries while I chatted with my friends here."

One of the uniformed cops picked up a spoon and poked at the uneaten bowl of chili. "This one's got beans."

Crissy covered her face with her hands. "God. What's happening? Who would want to do this to me?"

The detective looked grim. "That's something we need to figure out." He rubbed his jaw. "I'll need to link up with my counterparts in Palm Dunes, and since this looks like a crime that's crossed district lines, we'll probably have to bring in the state." He pinned each of us with a stare. "Make sure we have your contact information."

"How could this have happened at the Riptide?" Crissy was anguished. "I've been playing this place as long as they've had live music. No one here hates me."

"We talked to the kitchen staff and the servers, as well as the night manager. The owner came over, too. Everyone checks out. They're just kids in the kitchen, and they're terrified. Wait staff's all been here for years. Same with the manager."

"So it's got to be someone from outside." Crissy frowned. "I thought when Maddy . . . it was just some sick, crazy person, and no one was targeting anyone. But this means it's me. Someone hates me enough to make me want to die—like that." She swallowed hard.

"You can't think of anyone who hates you? Any other, ah, singers or whatever who might be jealous?"

"Absolutely not." Crissy shook her head. "I know a few other performers, but we're not like that. Everyone supports each other. We're happy for our successes."

"Still, I'd like a list of names, just to be thorough."

It was another hour before we were allowed to leave. Lucas and I walked toward our car with Rafe and Nell.

"I'm sorry this evening turned out to be an attempted-murder." Lucas tightened his grip on my hand as he spoke to Rafe.

"Hey, never a dull moment with you two. And how could you have known? You're not a seer or a mind hearer."

"No." Lucas was silent for a minute, his mouth set in a grim line, and I remembered his reaction when we'd been introduced to Dell.

"What did you see with Dell? You reacted. I felt it."

Lucas cast his eyes down to me. "Yeah, I know." He sighed. "I heard his number. His death age. And it was lower than I'd have expected."

Rafe and Nell exchanged glances. They knew, as I did, that part of being a death broker meant hearing the death age or the time left of nearly every person Lucas met. The numbers he heard varied; sometimes it was the exact age of their death, and sometimes it was how long they had left. He was often able to block the knowledge, and if the person had any type of extraordinary gift, he didn't hear the information. He also didn't hear my number, though we weren't sure exactly why that was the case.

"What about Trina?" Rafe hooked his thumbs in the front pockets of his jeans. "What was her number?"

"Much higher than what her age is now. So I wasn't completely worried, even when she was poisoned."

"But maybe someone needs to warn Dell." Rafe stopped behind his vintage Impala. "If it looks like he's the next one in danger, and you know it . . ." His voice trailed off, but we all knew what he meant.

"How can I do that? Just call up Crissy and say, 'Hey, not to sound weird or anything, but your guitarist is probably next on the kill list. Tell him to watch his steps.'" Lucas blew out a long breath. "She'd think I was insane or worse, that I was the one behind the poisonings."

"I imagine the police are going to warn everyone involved with Crissy to be vigilant." Nell spoke matter-of-factly. "Two of her known associates have been targeted, or at the very least, have been collateral damage in someone's quest to kill Crissy. They'll all be told to be more careful. Probably advised not to eat anything that they don't make themselves."

"Nell's right." I nodded. "And even if you did warn Dell, there's no guarantee he'd . . . well, the numbers are pretty much set in stone, aren't they?"

"I've never tried to save anyone whose number is—uh, coming up, not to sound flippant. I'd have to find out how old

Dell is now to be sure how close the end is. Would've been nice if I'd heard the time left instead of his death age. Gotta love having a gift you can't control."

"I hear you, man." Rafe sounded resigned "All we can do is keep our eyes open and hope for the best at this point. Let us know if there's anything we can do on our end."

"Are you driving all the way back to Carruthers tonight?" Harper Creek, the Institute's headquarters, was at least a three-hour drive from where we were.

"No, we've got a room waiting for us at the hotel we investigated last month. They've comped us for all time, apparently." Rafe opened the passenger door for Nell. "Care to come with us? They've probably got a couple of vacancies."

"Thanks, but we've got a canine kid waiting for us at home." Lucas laid a hand on my shoulder. "We'll take a rain check, though."

I gave Rafe a quick hug as he rounded the car to the driver's side. "Thank you again for listening to me. And talking to me."

"Any time, gorgeous." He smirked, shooting a teasing glance at Lucas. "You know, if I wasn't crazy in love with the witch in the car, I'd persuade you to ditch the death broker and run off with me. End of the world or not."

"Hey, hey. Get moving, buddy. This one's taken. Go on, get out of here and go save the world." His smile faded a little. "I'll be up in a few weeks for the next meeting."

"See you then, man. Safe travels." He walked backward a few steps, and with his fingers on the door handle, sketched a salute in our direction. "And hey, watch what you eat. It'd be pretty ironic if the death broker was poisoned."

Chapter 8

"I WANT TO TALK with you about what happened with Delia."

We were speeding down the highway through the dark, taking the shorter route back to Palm Dunes now that the sun had set. For the first fifteen minutes of the ride, neither of us spoke beyond the small necessities of regulating the car's temperature and finding the right radio station. But I knew I had to talk to Lucas now, tonight, or I'd chicken out.

When I spoke into the dimly-lit interior of the car, I didn't look at him. I kept my eyes on the road in front of us.

"Okay." There was no judgment there, no expectation.

"When Delia took over, it was scary. I felt like I was going to die. I told you that. She came in, and it was like someone was climbing into a dress I was already wearing. Only instead of the dress ripping, she just . . . pushed me deeper. Down far, so far that I couldn't breathe or think or even exist anymore. I ceased to be for that space of time."

Lucas didn't say anything, but his hands tightened on the steering wheel.

"And I thought that was bad, but then awareness started to come back. And that was even worse. Because as I came back, it meant I was pushing Delia out since the two of us could not fit in my body. But doing that felt wrong. She was holding on with everything she had, trying to fight you from removing her and fighting me from taking over again. She . . . she screamed, Lucas, and it was the most horrific thing I've ever heard. She begged me not to make her go. She said she didn't want to go back. When she was torn away, it felt like she scraped off a piece of my soul."

After a moment of silence, Lucas reached for my hand. "I'm sorry. I had no idea. I knew she didn't want to go, but I didn't know she'd hung on. And I didn't know you'd been hurt."

"I didn't want to talk about it, because I felt so guilty. For sending her back. How could I do that?"

"How could you not? Jackie, you said it yourself. There wasn't room for both of you. You did what you needed to do to survive. No one blames you for doing it, and you shouldn't blame yourself. Besides, it was really me who forced Delia back to the gray place."

"I know that logically. But it still feels as though it was me who did it. And sometimes I can still hear her. In my dreams, too."

"Why didn't you tell me?" Lucas steered the car to the exit that would lead us to Palm Dunes. "I might've been able to help you."

"I didn't want you to think I blamed you. I don't. And I needed to figure it out myself."

"Talking to Rafe helped?"

I hesitated. "Some, yes, but it wasn't so much talking to him. It was . . . he gave me a choice. I could keep the memory, terrible as it was, or I could get rid of it. I could have him remove it, and then I'd be free. I think it was the idea of being able to make the decision myself. Having that small measure of control, when Delia had taken all of it away from me."

Lucas turned into Golden Rays. "But you decided not to have him do it? To take them away?"

I shook my head. "No. I want to keep them, because they may end up to be important, and I think not getting rid of them was the wiser choice."

He shot me a wide smile. "It's the brave choice, without doubt."

The warmth of his approval spread through me. "It might take me a little while to completely make my peace with what happened with Delia, but I think I'm on the right track." I laced my fingers through his. "Talking to you helps. I'm sorry I didn't do it before."

"You had to do things in your own time. I understand." The car bumped into his driveway, and after shifting into park, he pulled the keys from the ignition. Silence surrounded us.

I unbuckled my seat belt and turned to face Lucas. "Thank you for being so patient with me about needing time in other areas, too. Lots of guys wouldn't have been so nice about it." I wriggled my skirt up and swung one leg over his lap, straddling him, with my back to the steering wheel.

"What's this?" His eyes gleamed in the dark, and his hands skimmed up my ribs.

"This is me, saying I'm ready." I braced my hands on his shoulders and ground my center against the ridge under the fly of his jeans, the one that was growing at an encouraging rate the more I wiggled.

"Are you sure?" Lucas moved his hands so that his thumbs teased the bottom of my breasts, sending a line of fire down my body. Maybe my mind had been on a sex hiatus for the last week or so, but clearly my body was ready to rock and roll.

"I'm sure." I rocked forward so that my nipples drilled into his palms. "Don't I feel ready?"

"You feel fucking amazing." He grasped the back of my neck with one hand and pushed my mouth to his, sealing his lips across mine as his tongue plunged between them. Yeah, he was definitely on board with this plan.

"So do you." I snaked my hand between us, stroking at his erection, and Lucas hissed in a breath.

"Should we move this inside?" He shoved his fingers under my shirt, fumbling with the cups of my bra.

"No." I tugged up his T-shirt, skimming over his chest and abdomen. "I've never had sex in a car before. I think this is the perfect time."

"You know I love to introduce you to new things." He

grasped the hem of my shirt and lifted it. “Take this off.”

I twisted and did as he said, only getting it caught on my earring once. Lucas curled his fingers around the lacy cups of my bra and pulled them until my nipples were exposed to his mouth and his tongue.

“I love the taste of you here.” His lips moved against my heated skin as he whispered. “Different here than anywhere else.”

“Feels good.” I managed the words on a gasp. “Oh, God, so good.”

Lucas moved his mouth to the other breast and at the same time, pushed my skirt out of the way so that his fingers could reach between my legs. He slid one teasing finger beneath my underwear and into my folds, touching me everywhere but where I most needed him.

“You’re so wet. So ready. Tell me what you want, baby. Do you want me to stop? Want me to touch you somewhere else?”

“No.” I moaned and shifted, trying to get him to find the right spot. “Don’t stop. Harder. And—” I grasped his wrist and moved it so that his finger hit the small button of nerves that craved his touch. “There. Right there. Oh, God, keep going.”

He replaced his finger with his thumb and slid two slick fingers inside me, pumping them faster as my hips pinioned. I gripped his arms and rode his hand until pleasure exploded into shimmery, shiny stars that fell over us both.

I collapsed against his chest, touching my lips to his neck, tasting his desire and feeling the rapid beat of his pulse. Lucas ran his hands down my spine and cupped my ass.

"God, that was incredible." I traced a circle on his clavicle with my tongue. "And now I want you inside me."

I walked my fingers down his stomach to the button of his jeans, flicked it open and eased down the zipper. He lifted his hips so I could free his cock, and I fisted it, moving my hand up and down, stroking the smooth hardness until he groaned and gripped my hips.

"I need you now, baby. God, I need to be in you."

I raised up and reached to slip my underwear aside. Lucas positioned himself at my entrance, sliding just slightly inside me. I eased down, inch by agonizing inch, until I was fully impaled on his erection.

And then I started to move.

Being on top was never comfortable for me in bed; it always felt like I was just missing the right spot, the right rhythm. But somehow this angle, in this small space where movement was limited, was perfect. I moved my hips in a way that sent a shot of pure pleasure through me. It must've felt pretty good to Lucas, too, since he moaned my name and jerked up in reaction.

"Let me . . ." He cupped one breast and lifted the nipple to his mouth as I continued to ride him. He sucked hard, worrying the sensitive bud between his teeth. His breath sped up, and I knew he was almost there.

"Love you, Jackie. Being in you is fucking perfect. God, baby, I'm close."

He dropped his mouth back to my breast, but this time, his teeth sank into me just beyond the areola, and he sucked hard. I cried out in surprise, but the bite was more sensual than painful, and I writhed, coming hard for the second time.

Lucas released my breast, made a noise deep in his throat and thrust upwards, his body one huge, tensing muscle. I held onto him, whispering soft words of love as both of us caught our breath.

"So first time in a car. I popped your car cherry." He kissed my neck just below my ear. "How was it?"

"Oh, I guess it was okay."

"Just okay?" He poked at my ribs until I was gasping with laughter and begging for mercy.

"All right, all right, it was wonderful. Perfect." I sat up and kissed him, long and hard, enjoying the feel of him still inside me. "The boob bite was new."

I felt him tense a little. "Sorry. I couldn't . . . well, usually it's your thigh. That muscle that drives me crazy. But I couldn't reach it, and so . . ." One shoulder lifted. "Instinct."

"Not complaining. It was hot."

I felt his lips curve. "Good. I was aiming for hot." He nuzzled my neck. "Should we go inside?"

"Or we could go . . . again, here." I rubbed against him.

"Hmmmm." He pulled me tighter against him, and just as I began to feel a new tremor of want, a bright light blinded me.

"Who's in there? Jackie? Lucas? Is that you?"

"Oh my God, it's Mrs. Ackers." Lucas's neighbor on the other side was infamous for her chronic insomnia. Clearly she'd been looking out her window and seen the car. And she'd probably seen movement in the car, and being the good neighbor that she was, she'd come down to investigate.

Lucas cursed eloquently and pulled me with him as he slid

down. "Maybe she'll just go away if we hide. And ignore her. Just be really quiet."

His voice sounded so funny as he tried to be quiet, and the combination of that with the ludicrous situation struck me as incredibly funny. My body shook with laughter as we sunk lower until Lucas was almost flat on the seat.

"Lucas, she saw us. We can't hide."

"We can. And we will."

"She's not going to go away. She can't sleep, she's bored and she's got nothing better to do than wait us out. So we can lay here like this until sunrise, or we can sit up and face the music."

"Music I'm okay with. Mrs. Ackers, not so much."

"My leg's going to sleep. Hand me my shirt." I managed to get it over my head and fixed the cups of my bra, then started to pull myself off Lucas. "Here, just—"

"Jackie, don't move. If you roll off me, Mrs. Ackers is going to an eyeful of more than she expected."

"Hey, what if I just cover you with my skirt until you zip up?" Without waiting for him to answer, I shifted, lifting off him and balancing on my arms until he tugged up his pants and fastened them.

"Okay, I'm good." He sounded a little less freaked out.

"Let's get out of the car, then." I made to reach for the door.

"Wait." Lucas gripped my arm. "Why don't *you* just get out and walk Mrs. Ackers home? And once you're far enough away, I'll get out and go inside. I'll meet you in your house."

"Why do I have to do it?"

"Because. You can convince her it was just you in the car, maybe. Tell her you were just . . . I don't know, listening to the radio. Having some 'you' time."

I rolled my eyes. "Because I take my 'me' time in a car at midnight? She's not going to buy it. And get real, Lucas. She saw you. She probably saw both of us being, um, us in a very unique way. Get over it, honey—there are no more secrets from Mrs. Ackers."

He groaned. "How am I going to face her again?"

"You're about to find out. Sitting here while she's standing out there waving around that flashlight is only making it worse. Pretty soon, someone else is going to wake up, and before you know it, we'll have a block party. Let's minimize the damage while we can."

I didn't give him any more opportunity to argue. Grabbing the door handle, I pushed it open and pasted on a bright smile.

"Hey, Mrs. Ackers! Everything all right?"

Mrs. Ackers was not my favorite neighbor. There was a rumor in Golden Rays that she kept a pair of high-powered binoculars on the table next to her window, and I believed it. During the period of time after Lucas's aunt had passed and before he'd moved in, when there was nothing but an empty house between us, she'd taken to wandering over any time she saw me outside. And she wasn't fun like Mrs. Mac; no, Mrs. Ackers felt it was her duty to point out all of my shortcomings and steer me on the straight-and-narrow. Her advice ranged from dog training (Makani was just a baby puppy then) to the flowers in my garden (never a high priority in my life) to how many lights I left on at night.

Since Lucas had moved in, I'd gotten a slight reprieve, since he was now around to distract her from me. She'd made no secret of her disapproval of our relationship, saying we were setting a poor example by cavorting out in the open, not even bothering to try to hide the fact that Lucas spent most nights at my house. I wasn't sure for whom we were setting that bad example, since we were the youngest two residences in the community, and let me tell you, what went on among the senior set was far more scandalous than what happened between Lucas and me. Until tonight, anyway.

"No, Jackie, everything is *not* all right. I was sleeping soundly, and you know how rare that is for me, with my insomnia—" She paused, giving me time to appreciate the tragedy of her sleep issues. "And I was awakened by a terrible racket coming from over here. I glanced out my window—" *With her binoculars, no doubt.* "—and saw *movement* in this car. Well, naturally, I assumed something nefarious was going on. Some young delinquents breaking into Lucas's car. So imagine my shock when I came over here to investigate and saw–" Her lips pursed together, like she'd just swallowed a lemon. "—what I saw. Shameful, the both of you."

I cast a backward glance at Lucas, who was still sitting in the driver's seat, staring straight ahead, pretending Mrs. Ackers and I didn't exist. Or maybe pretending he was driving far, far away.

"Mrs. Ackers, you know, if you suspected a crime, you should've called the police. It's not safe for you to be out in the middle of the night, confronting possible criminals. Why, what if there really had been a break-in? You might've been seriously hurt." I tried to steer the conversation to what might have happened and away from what really had, but she was having none of it.

"It's bad enough that you two tromp between each other bedrooms with no regard for what's right, but now you're copulating out in the open? In automobiles?" She shook her head.

Lucas finally climbed out of the car, jamming his hands deep in the front pockets of his jeans. "Mrs. Ackers, you should probably go home. It's late, and it's chilly. Would you like me to walk you to your door?"

She drew herself up and shook her head. "No, thank you. I'm perfectly capable of getting home by myself." She narrowed her eyes and planted her hands on her hips. "And I'll thank you both to conduct yourself with a little more decorum."

With that parting shot, Mrs. Ackers marched down the driveway, swinging her flashlight in self-righteous indignation. I sighed and shook my head.

"Well, that's it. She'll be up at the crack of dawn, making sure everyone in the neighborhood knows we were getting busy in your car. I'm going to have to move."

Lucas closed his hand around my neck and leaned to kiss me, his lips searing mine and reminding me exactly why we'd been hot and heavy in the front seat. I stood on my toes and linked my hands behind his head, holding him to me. He traced a line to my ear with his mouth, the warmth of his breath making me shiver.

"Before you start packing up for that move, why don't

we move this party to your bed? I think we've got a little more catching up to do."

Chapter 9

AS I'D PREDICTED, the tale of our midnight lovin' was already making the rounds of the neighborhood by the time I dragged myself out of bed the next morning. Mrs. Mac, who'd been sulking about Lucas's tight lips in the Maddy affair, found it in herself to forgive both of us and was at the back door before noon, eager to tell us what was being said.

"Mrs. Ackers says you were doing kinky stuff, like in that movie I made you watch." Delighted humor danced in my friend's eyes. "I want to hear all about it."

I groaned. "That is so *not* true. We weren't—I mean, we *were*, but not like that. Just . . . you know, normal, everyday type of . . . stuff."

"If you're going to do it, honey, you need to be able to say it!" Mrs. Mac crowed and then collapsed into helpless laughter. "Oh, Jackie. I just wish I'd been there to see the look on your face. Oh, and Lucas's, too. Where is he, anyway? Mortified? Off hiding?"

"No." I shook my head. "He, ah, got called into . . . an appointment early this morning. He'd forgotten he had it." The truth was, of course, that he'd been called to a Reckoning earlier and hadn't returned yet. I was getting a little worried; Reckonings usually didn't take him very long. It wasn't a long process; Lucas showed up, as did the advocates, they each gave their reasoning for why the soul should be moved to one place or another, Lucas made his pronouncement and that was that. And once the soul had been sent to its destination, Lucas was transported back to wherever he'd been when he left. The whole deal was out of his hands, and the traveling was automatic. It wasn't like he could stop on the way home to pick up a six-pack, so I had to assume something unexpected had gone down.

"Well, he'll have to come out of hiding sooner or later. And you can tell him I consider this payback for him not coming clean with me about that murder. I could've had the scoop before everyone else, but no, he had to be close-mouthed and discreet. Do you know who I had to hear about Maddy's murder from? Nancy Gray. Do you know how humiliating that was?"

Actually, I did. Nancy Gray was a lovely woman, one of the leaders in the Golden Rays community. She had a sweet husband whom she loved and who doted on her, children and grandchildren who visited frequently and a beautiful home with a garden that was the envy of the neighborhood. And she was Mrs. Mac's arch enemy.

Not that Nancy Gray knew it, of course. But Mrs. Mac couldn't stand Nancy, and because of that, hearing juicy gossip from the other woman was particularly painful.

"I'm sorry, Mrs. Mac. But hey, I can make it up to you now. Did you hear about the incident up in Crystal Cove last night? One of Crissy Darwin's best friends was poisoned, and Lucas and I were there."

Her eyes went wide. "Is she dead?"

"No, not as far as I know. She was rushed to the hospital, but I think they were able to save her."

"Oh." Mrs. Mac looked disappointed for a moment before she remembered herself. "Not that I'd want anyone to die, of course. But getting the skinny on an attempted murder isn't the same as finding out the details on a real murder."

"Sorry. I'll have to work a little harder to make sure I'm at the more happening deaths in Palm Dunes."

She waved her hand in the air. "Not your fault." She winked at me. "Of course, if you're too busy having sex in cars, you won't get any hot gossip for me. I guess in that case, you *are* the hot gossip."

I closed my eyes. *Kill me now.* "Thanks, Mrs. Mac."

"No problem. I've got to go. The girls and I are meeting to finalize the plans for our craft booth at the Festival. See you later, gator."

I dropped into a kitchen chair and covered my face with

my hands, hoping and praying that no one from Palm Dunes had my mother's phone number or email address. The last thing I needed was this story going viral in my New York hometown.

"Jackie."

I jumped a mile when Lucas said my name. After all this time, I should've been more used to him popping in and out of my house, but for some reason, I never was.

"God, you scared the hell out of me." I stood up and wrapped my arms around his waist, kissing his jaw. "You were gone a long time. I was starting to worry."

"I know. Well, it was complicated." He stroked my hair down my back and then sat, pulling me onto his lap. "Jackie, it was Dell."

For a minute, I was lost. *Dell?* The only Dell I knew was the one we'd met last night. And then it hit me.

"Shit."

"Yeah, pretty much." He swallowed, his Adam's apple moving in his throat.

"Another poisoning?"

"Not this time." He looked grim. "Dell was killed with an ax."

My stomach churned. "Oh, my God. That's horrible."

"It really was."

"Where? And how?"

Lucas brushed his hand over my thigh. "At his house. In his backyard. There were signs of a struggle. And the how . . . well, just take my word for it. That ax blade was buried deep."

"Yeah, I don't need to know any more details. I can't

imagine what it was like for you to see him."

"And after the Reckoning—which wasn't much fun, either—I hung around to see what was going to happen."

I lifted one eyebrow. "Really? Weren't you worried about being seen at yet another crime scene connected with this case? I understand you've got some kind of nifty supernatural protection, but why would you put it to the test?"

Lucas shook his head. "It wasn't like I had a choice. I just didn't transport. This time, the light advocate was able to cloak me, and he stayed with me while we watched the police work."

"I can't believe this." I rested my head on Lucas's shoulder. "Do they know who did it? The police, I mean?"

"Not really. Murder weapon was partially missing—the ax handle was gone. They're assuming it's connected with the two poisonings, and one of the detectives wondered if Dell suspected who had killed Maddy and tried to kill Trina. If he confronted the person . . . maybe he panicked and killed Dell, to protect his own secret."

"God, that's horrible."

"I know. And I kept thinking, I knew it was going to happen. What could I have done to stop it? If I'd said something to him last night, even if he thought I was nuts, maybe he would've been more careful."

"Lucas, you don't know that. If he really did have an idea of who the murderer is, he could've said something to the police. He had choices. And if that's not the case, if it was just a random killing, nothing you could've done would change that."

He sighed. "I hear you, but I can't help feeling guilty."

"I know." I stroked his stubbly cheek. He'd been summoned to the Reckoning this morning before he even had time to shave.

"On the other hand, I think this confirms that someone's after Crissy. Or at the very least, someone is trying to isolate her by getting rid of all the people closest to her. I heard one of the detectives suggest that her parents and friends be notified that they could be in danger."

My heart was heavy. She was so young to be dealing with all this loss. "Poor Crissy. She must be devastated. Dell's been playing with her for a long time. He's been at the last three Festivals with her."

"Do you think we should text her? Just to give her our condolences?"

Lucas shook his head. "We can't now. The story hasn't broken, and so technically, we don't know about Dell yet."

"Oh, that's right. Damn, it sucks to have the insider info and not be able to share it. Or use it." I sat quietly for a few beats. "Which reminds me . . . Mrs. Mac was here this morning. She said to tell you Mrs. Ackers catching us in the act gets you off the hook for not telling her more about Maddy's murder. She was getting quite the chuckle out of us. Apparently we're the big story of the day at Golden Rays."

Lucas dropped his head onto my shoulder. "Shoot me now."

I gave him a light punch. "Hey, what're you worried about? No one's going to call your family and rat you out. Do you know how many people in Palm Dunes know my parents? Too many."

He went pale. "Didn't you tell me your parents were coming down here for Christmas?"

"You know they are. We talked about taking them to the beach for a weekend if it's nice enough."

"So your dad might be here, knowing that I was banging his little girl in my car in the middle of the night?"

"'Fraid so."

Lucas groaned. "I'm so screwed. I need to start going door-to-door around the neighborhood, bribing every one of the old gossips not to tell anyone."

"Good luck, honey. If you start now, you might have a fighting chance."

Lucas and I spent most of the rest of that day watching the news, waiting for Dell's murder to be reported. Lucas stretched out on the couch and napped a little; Reckonings always took a lot out of him. I called the diner to check in and reported to Mary that I'd finalized the recipe for my pie entry.

"Oh, honey, that's wonderful news. I can't wait. Do you want me to come over and do a taste test?"

I laughed. "There's a waiting list for that job at this point, but thanks. I hope you'll like it. I really don't want to let Leone's down."

"Jackie." Mary's tone lost all humor. "You don't seriously

think you could ever disappoint any of us at the diner, do you? You saved this place. If you hadn't agreed to take it over after we lost Al, God only knows what might have become of us. I'd probably be playing shuffleboard down in Sarasota, hating every minute of it. We all want you to win the prize at the Triple P, and teach that Bitsy a lesson, but that's not what's important. It's one day out of the year. You're behind us every single day, and that's what matters."

A lump rose in my throat. "That's one of the sweetest things anyone's ever said to me. Thank you, Mary. I'm really grateful for all the support all of you have given me."

"Al would be proud of you. He used to tell me that if only you'd trust yourself, you'd be an excellent chef. 'One day, Mary,' he'd say, 'one day our Jackie'll realize what makes her heart sing, and she'll amaze everyone. When that happens, I'm going to make her come cook with me.'"

Tears filled my eyes. "I never knew that. I had no idea he wanted me to cook with him."

"Sure, he thought the cookbook would be the first step in that direction." She sniffed. "He sure was excited about it. Every time someone comes into the diner and buys one of those books, I think he's smiling down on us."

"I think so, too. I gave a copy to Crissy Darwin the other day. Did you know she and Al were friends?"

Mary laughed. "Jackie, if I tried to keep track of all the people who Al befriended, I wouldn't have time to keep this place running. That's just how he was. He had a knack for making every person he knew feel like she was the most important one in his life. It's a gift."

Across the room, on the side table, Lucas's phone began to buzz. I glanced at him, still sacked out on the couch, and stood up to get it.

"Mary, I'm sorry, but the other phone is ringing. I'll stop in tomorrow before we head for the Festival, okay?"

"Sure thing, honey. I'll see you then."

I disconnected that call and answered Lucas's phone. "Hello?"

"Jackie? Is that you?" The voice on the end was thick with emotion. "This is Crissy. I was just calling . . ." She drew in a shaky breath. "I'm afraid I have some really bad news."

As she spoke, the four o'clock news came on the television, with the lead story the murder of local musician Dell Jamison.

"Oh, my God, Crissy." I wanted to save her the added pain of having to say the words. "I'm seeing it on TV right now. I can't believe . . . Dell. Are you—well, I know you're not all right. What can we do?"

"Could you . . . is there any way you could come over? You and Lucas? I know that sounds weird. I mean, I haven't known you very long, but I'm just, um, alone right now. Trina's still in the hospital, and Maddy—" Crissy's voice broke on a sob.

"Of course, we'll come over right now. Where are you?"

"I'm at my parents' house. I'll text you the address. Thank you so much, Jackie. I can't tell you how much it means to me."

I shook Lucas awake. "Hey, sleepyhead. That was Crissy on the phone."

His eyes flew open. "What? Is she okay?" He pushed himself to sit up.

"She wants us to come over. Why don't you get changed and I'll drive us? You still look exhausted."

"I am. I think the extra time on the scene must've sapped my energy."

Crissy's parents lived in Seminole Falls, about fifteen minutes away. I found their home without issue and turned down a long driveway.

"Ma'am, I need to see some ID." A uniformed police officer stepped up to the car before we could get out. "And I'll have to call into the house to see if the family wants to see you."

As Lucas and I both fumbled to pull out our driver's licenses, the front door of the house opened and Crissy stepped out.

"It's okay. I called them to come over. Please just let them come in."

The cop gave us a brief nod and stood back as Lucas and I opened the car doors and climbed the few steps to the front porch.

"Crissy, I'm so sorry." Lucas gave her a brief hug.

"Thank you for coming over. I told Jackie on the phone, I know it's strange to feel this way when I've just met you, but I don't . . . everyone else is gone." Her whole body quivered, as though she was holding back an enormous sob.

"I can't even imagine." I squeezed her arm. "And it's not strange. When you get to know people during times of stress, sometimes things escalate. It's not always how long you've been acquainted with someone that determines how deep those feelings are."

"Exactly." Crissy wiped at her cheeks. "God, I can't seem to stop crying. And we're standing out here on the front porch. Come on in."

The house was not huge or ostentatious. The living room we stepped into was warm and comfortable, with furniture that had definitely seen better days, although it was still serviceable. The neighborhood itself was older and filled with typical middle-class-type houses; they were well-cared for, but not new or ostentatious by any means. It didn't seem that Crissy's rising star was translating into money yet.

As we all sat down, an older version of Crissy came into the room. The tired smile she wore looked pasted on.

"Hello. I'm Rachel Darwin, Crissy's mom. Thank you for coming. Crissy . . . she needs all her friends right now."

"Being my friend right now means risking your life." Crissy shot the words back. "Everyone who gets close to me ends up dead."

"That's not true. Trina's going to be fine. This is just . . . some horrible coincidence."

Crissy snorted. "Yeah, coincidence. Mom, the police agree someone's targeting me. Maddy and Dell are dead. *Dead.* Trina's in the hospital after almost dying. And all of that's because they knew me. Because they worked with me. They don't have anyone or anything else in common." She slammed her hand down on the pillow in the corner of the sofa. "Don't try to make me feel better."

Rachel rubbed her forehead and glanced at me. "I'm sorry. We're all a little overwrought right now."

"Understandable." I looked at Crissy. "Did the police—are there any theories yet? I mean, Dell . . . it wasn't poison. Seems unusual for a killer to change his MO."

"They said what happened with Dell looked like some kind of fight. One of the detectives thinks it's possible Dell was suspicious of someone, confronted him about it, and the killer attacked him outside his back door." She shrugged. "Of course, the other detective believes it was just a random murder, that maybe he interrupted a robbery or something. Which is stupid, because nothing was taken but the ax handle and Dell's cell phone, which does more to support the first theory." She buried her face in her hands. "When I think about it . . . about him dying that way . . ."

"Crissy, don't." Rachel sat on the arm of the couch and drew her daughter close. "Don't torture yourself." She met my eyes. "She was getting so upset, we were going to call the doctor about giving her a sedative. But she said she'd rather talk to you two, that she needed friends, not meds."

"I have to make sense of this whole mess somehow. Jackie, you've been to my shows for years. Did I ever do something or say something on stage that would make anyone want to hurt me? Who would hate me this much?"

"I'm sure it's nothing you've done or said. This person, whoever it is, has got to be insane. And the police will catch him. They're offering you protection?"

She nodded. "The detective thinks it's important, especially for my mom and dad. They're the closest people to me."

"And you're staying here with them?"

"For the time being. It's easier for us to watch out for each other. We're not eating any food from outside our own kitchen, no take-out. They're monitoring who comes into the house, and none of us are going out alone."

"It's only until they catch this maniac. Then life will go back to normal." Rachel kissed the top of Crissy's head. "It's temporary."

"Nothing's ever going to be normal again. If this is the cost for my career, I don't want it. I can't stand the idea that my singing made this happen."

"Oh, honey." Her mother shot me a pleading look. "Crissy's saying she thinks she needs to pull out of the pecan festival. The police said it was fine for her to perform, and her father and I think she needs to do it."

"Don't you think it would be insensitive to Dell's memory to be back on stage two days after he's brutally murdered? God, I can't even think of it. I haven't performed without him in over three years. I'm not sure I can."

"We can find someone to play for you." She smiled a little. "Or you could do it. Remember when you first started, you always played for yourself."

Crissy shook her head, but I noticed that her shoulders relaxed a little. "I'm not very good, Mom."

"But I bet no one else knows your songs the way you do." Lucas leaned forward. "Although, if you want the support . . . I play guitar."

I turned to him, my mouth dropping open. "You do? Since when?"

The corner of his mouth lifted a little. "Since always.

Well, since I was about ten years old. I was even in a band for a while in college."

Crissy clasped her hands together. "Would you seriously consider it? I know it's last minute, but my music isn't that hard to learn. I think I could go up on stage if someone I knew was with me. I wouldn't feel so alone, you know?"

That's how it happened that when we walked out the door of the Darwin home an hour later, Lucas had a gig at the Triple P Festival.

"How did I not know this about you?" I tossed him the keys over the hood of the car. "You're awake now. You drive home."

He caught them and opened the driver's side door. "I guess it just never came up. We've been a little busy in the last year, haven't we? I'm sure you have tons of stuff about yourself that I don't know." He winked at me as I climbed into the car. "That's why I plan to spend a lot of time with your folks and with Leesa when they come down for the holidays. I need to get the whole scoop on all things Jackie."

"Thanks. That'll be fun." I slid him a side-eyed glance. "Maybe you can fit all that in after you explain to my dad about Mrs. Ackers catching us in the act in your car."

Lucas groaned. "Okay, okay, point taken. I promise, no digging."

"So back to your hidden guitar talents. You're actually pretty good."

He smirked. "Thanks for that ringing endorsement."

"No, I mean, for someone who hasn't played as long as I've known him. Why haven't you? When did you stop?"

He lifted one shoulder and backed the car out of the driveway. “About the time I moved to Florida. Matter of fact, the last night I played was at the bar where we had my farewell party. I jammed with a few of my friends right before I met Veronica.”

I bit my lip. As far as we knew, Veronica was the name of the vampire who was responsible for Lucas for being one, too. He only vaguely remembered her, since he’d been totally drunk the night he met her, but she’d left him a cryptic note, one that Cathryn and several other experts at Carruthers had examined closely. We weren’t much closer to determining why he’d been changed, even though Veronica had claimed she’d intervened for a reason. Since his death broker abilities had appeared at the same time, Cathryn felt the two had to be connected.

“Will you play for me some time? I mean, I know I’ll hear you tomorrow night with Crissy, but having a man play just for me is kind of a fantasy of mine.”

His eyebrows shot up. “Seriously? How did I not know this? Baby, I’ll play for you tonight. I’ll play for you every damn night.”

I laughed softly. “I’m living out fantasies left and right this week. First the car, now the guitar . . . I’m going to have to start coming up with some new ones.”

“Jackie, babe, I’m here for you. More than willing to help you with that kind of research.”

“You’re too good to me.” I was quiet for a few minutes as we drove through the night. “Lucas, are you sure it’s a good idea for you to be up there on stage with Crissy? Will it be safe?"

"Safer for me than anyone else, right? Vampire and death broker hybrid here."

"We don't know anything about you being either immortal or invincible, buddy. I'm not excited about putting those two things to the test."

"I can help Crissy. She'll feel better having me up there, and maybe I can help keep her safe, too. I was afraid she was going to cancel on the Triple P Festival if I didn't agree to do it."

"But you'll be careful, right? You'll keep your eyes open, not eat anything? And watch out for ax-wielding crazies?"

"Of course I will. Hey, I don't have a death wish." He reached across the console and gripped my hand. "If nothing else, I have all those sexual fantasies to help you realize. That's enough reason for me to live."

"You're too good to me." I lifted our joined hands and kissed his knuckles.

"I'm nothing if not a giver."

Chapter 10

"IS IT SAFE to come in, or do I need to be blindfolded?" Lucas stood in the living room, just outside the kitchen, one hand over his eyes.

"Oh, just come in, you goof. I trust you not to blab about my entry. Especially since I just took the winning pie out of the oven." I set down the oven mitts and leaned against the counter, crossing my arms over my chest.

Lucas wandered in, sniffing the air. "Well, it definitely smells amazing." He spied the pie on the counter, and his eyes grew wide. "Is that . . ."

"Yep." I nodded, bracing for his reaction.

"Wow. That's just . . . it's wild." He walked around, checking it out from all sides. "It's actually kind of amazing."

"Thanks. Let's hope the judges think so, too."

"They will. I have a good feeling about this."

"From your lips, buddy. Have you heard from Crissy at all?"

"She texted me this morning, just telling me where to meet her and what time. I told her we'd be there early anyway, so you could have the pie on site for the judging."

"That sounds good. I can't believe—" The doorbell rang, interrupting my next thought and setting Makani on a barking rant as he raced to the front door to protect Lucas and me from whatever doom might be waiting on the other side.

"Okay, killer, settle down. I promise to let you attack if it's an enemy." Lucas headed for the door and scooped up the frantic pup. "Seriously, Makani, chill. It's just . . ." He opened the door. "Cathryn."

My heart sank down to the bottom of my stomach. It was clear from the tone of Lucas's voice that the visit from his sort-of boss and ex-girlfriend was unexpected, which was very unusual for Cathryn Whitmore. She was a structured woman who, to the best of my knowledge, never acted impulsively or without careful planning. She always called before she came to see Lucas, which made think this was not a casual drop-by.

"I'm sorry for not calling." Cathryn confirmed my hunch right away. "I could say I didn't have time, which is partly true, but the truth is that I was afraid you'd tell me not to come, and this is too important to put off."

I rinsed off my hands and dried them on a tea towel as I walked into the living room. "Hello, Cathryn."

Her vibrant blue eyes flickered in my direction. "Jackie. You're doing . . . well?"

That was code for 'better', I knew. The last time I'd seen Cathryn, Lucas and I had been leaving Carruthers, and I was still shaky after the ritual.

I nodded. "Yes, thanks. Much better."

"I'm glad to hear it." She turned back to Lucas. "May I have just a few minutes of your time? I promise I won't keep you long."

"Sure." He spread out his hands. "Sit down." Taking a seat on the sofa, Lucas patted the cushion next to him and smiled at me. "Jackie?"

I joined him there, glancing at Cathryn. If she had any reaction to Lucas including me, she didn't show it. She sank into a winged chair, her back as straight as ever as she crossed her ankles and folded her hands in her lap.

"I know you saw Rafe and Nell the other day, but as I understand it, there wasn't much opportunity for discussion. Quite the eventful evening you had."

Lucas shrugged. "We're handling it. What's going on, Cathryn?"

She took a deep breath. "We've gotten some more information from our sources about what Delia told us. Everything has so far been confirmed. We haven't yet located the man in California, Mr. X, the leader of the commune, but we've found some of his associates. The few who are still alive, that is."

"Did they tell the same story? About what supposedly happened back in 1967?"

"All but one is severely demented and unable to communicate, but that one who could speak . . . yes. He's in a mental institute, and the doctors call him delusional, but in the context of what we learned about Mr. X, he's perfectly rational."

Lucas closed his eyes. "So it seems like it's true? This all started back then?"

Cathryn's smile was thin and humorless. "In the summer of love, yes. That's when the plan to end the world was set in motion. The irony isn't lost on any of us, believe me."

"What about the girl? Have you found her yet?" I hadn't heard Delia's story, since I was too busy being possessed by her at the time, nor had I been in any condition to understand it when Joss had recounted the details to the rest of the team, but Lucas had told me everything that they'd learned about the plot to destroy our world. Delia hadn't known everything, since she'd been a double agent, working for both Carruthers and the Hive at the time of her death. The leaders of the Hive hadn't entrusted her with all of their secrets.

What we did know, though, was that everything had begun decades before, on a small commune in northern California, during the heady days of the late 1960's. Somehow—and no one was certain about how this had happened—a group of young people on the commune had done something to open a door to another dimension. They'd been unable to finish what they'd started, but it had laid the groundwork for the Hive to take over and see it to the fateful destruction.

Delia had been hazy—or evasive—on the topic of their exact plans, but she did mention that their greatest fear was someone they called the Vessel, a young woman who possessed the ability to derail their plans. Cathryn had immediately begun investigating this Vessel, and finding her was a high priority.

Now she shook her head. "Unfortunately, no. Delia wasn't able to give us a location or a description. We don't know how old she is or even if she's in this country. Our researchers are working around the clock to figure out what that term means, but so far, it's just been dead-ends."

Lucas tensed his jaw. "Cathryn, did you drive all the way down here to tell us all the things you haven't figured out yet? Because it seems to me that could've been a telephone call."

"Of course not." Her voice was crisp. "I came down here for two reasons." She paused. "The first is to secure your commitment."

"Commitment?" He frowned. "What kind of commitment?"

"This fight is going to escalate fast, and winning it is going to take everything and everyone we have. So far, you've been operating as a sort of add-on agent at Carruthers. I appreciate that you came when I called a few weeks ago, and I'm confident that if I needed you on a short-term basis, you'd be there. But I need more than that. I want you to come on as a full-time agent, and I'd like you to do it as soon as possible."

Lucas drew his eyebrows together. "This is a big decision, Cathryn. It's not something I can jump into doing. Like you said, if you need me, all you have to do is call, and I'll be up there. What would change if I went full-time? I'm not moving up to Carruthers. Jackie and I have a life here. Friends. She owns a restaurant. We can't just move."

"I wouldn't expect you to move. Not all of our agents live

in the area. Julia, for instance. Our necroloquitar lives in New Jersey, as you know. We want that commitment to Carruthers because it means something. Making the decision means you've chosen a side. It means we can count on you to work tirelessly with the rest of us to prevent the destruction of life as we know it. I know it sounds odd, but the act of making that choice has intrinsic value. It's like the vows made by knights of old."

"You want me to swear fealty to you, Cathryn?" His lips twitched, but I knew none of us saw any humor in this scenario.

"I want you *both* to commit to Carruthers." For the first time, Cathryn looked me full in the face. "Jackie, this offer—or request, if you prefer—applies to you, too. We want you to also be an agent."

Shock made me jerk upright in my seat. "Me? But why? I don't have anything to offer you. I don't have any gifts or abilities. And I think it was made clear at the ritual that I'm more of liability than anything else."

"On the contrary." Cathryn traced a line at the edge of her skirt's hem, and I realized with surprise that she was nervous. I'd never seen her anything but completely self-assured. Even as I thought that, she met my gaze, and I remembered too late that her particular talent was hearing thoughts. *Damn.* When was I going to learn? I always ended up putting my proverbial foot in my mouth around this woman.

"What's that supposed to mean?" Lucas, oblivious to the undercurrent running between his ex-girlfriend and his current love, scowled at Cathryn.

Cathryn took a deep breath. "At the ritual, we realized that Jackie seems to have a vacuum of sorts. Being possessed by a soul is not common, not at all. And despite what popular movies portray, it can't happen to just anyone. None of the rest of us were viable options, but Delia was able to easily take over Jackie's body. If it happened before, it can happen again. And we might need that particular ability."

Lucas sprung to his feet. "Are you fucking kidding me, Cathryn? Did I not make it *clear* after that damned ritual that I didn't want Jackie anywhere near any of this shit again? And you want us to just agree to have her around in case a wandering spirit might need to use her body to have a chat with us? Just, 'oh, yeah, come right on in and take up residence. Sit down make yourself at home.'" He pointed at Cathryn. "Fuck, no. It's not going to happen."

"Would it help you win?" I spoke up, and my voice sounded eerily calm even to my own ears. "If I agree to allow this, would it help? Would it give the good guys an advantage?"

If I'd expected Cathryn to give me glowing assurances that I was needed, necessary and integral to winning the war and saving the world, I was disappointed. Cathryn Whitmore had many faults, I was sure, but exaggerating or padding the truth in order to get what she wanted was not one of them. In my experience, she was honest to a fault.

"Maybe." She lifted both of her shoulders. "We don't know. And would I be seeking your help if you weren't connected to Lucas?" She smiled a little. "Probably not. What you offer Carruthers has more value in the context of your relationship with Lucas than it would otherwise. But at this point, we're willing to do everything possible to give us an advantage." She leveled a stare at Lucas. "We're going to need all of it."

He swore under his breath.

I turned to face Cathryn. "I'll do it."

She closed her eyes, and her lips curved up a little. "Thank you."

Lucas glared at me. "I can't believe you. Do you understand what you're agreeing to do?"

I nodded. "Yeah, I'm agreeing to help save the world, however I can. I'm agreeing to fight on the same side as you. I love you, Lucas, and there's no way in hell or out of it that I'd let you march into this battle on your own. So I'm going as a page, not a knight." I reached out to take his hand. "I'm okay with that."

He sighed, but he didn't argue any more.

"All right, that's one." Cathryn was back to her brisk self. "The other reason I'm here involves Veronica."

Lucas tensed. "What did you find out?"

Cathryn's tongue darted out to lick her bottom lip. "All of our research had been far-flung, looking for her in the past, in reports from around the world. Checking all the typical sources and then the more unusual ones. As it turns out, I should've started a little closer to home." She gave a short, breathless laugh. "And the thing is, I knew it. Deep down, part of me knew it. I just didn't want to believe it."

"Would you care to be a little less cryptic, Cathryn? We're not following you." Lucas spoke through clenched teeth.

"Of course. I'm sorry." She faced Lucas full-on. "Veronica was—or is, I suppose—part of my family, my many-times-over great-grandmother. According to family legend, she disappeared shortly after her youngest child was born and was presumed to have been killed. She was a Carruthers."

Surprise made me gape. "How . . .? What does that mean? 'Presumed to have been killed?'"

Cathryn exhaled. "She was kidnapped from the family home. At the time, it was assumed that pirates were behind her vanishing, since the family was living on the coast of Spain, and piracy was rampant. But then several generations later, apparently, there were rumors that she'd been spotted. No one believed it was really her, of course, because she looked the same as when she'd disappeared, and the only people who would have truly remembered her were quite old with questionable memories and vision. But there are mentions here and there, throughout our family history, of stories that she was still alive and young. I never knew of them or of her.

"But when we were in Cape May, Lucas, that last night, I heard . . . something. At first I thought it was the ghost in the Inn, and then I realized it wasn't. She told me . . . things, and I probed, trying to figure out who or what she was. And I got the name Veronica. I don't think she counted on me doing that, because she was annoyed. Told me to pull it back, and then she told me—well, that doesn't matter. What does matter is that she mentioned you, Lucas, and she told me you had a destiny.

"When you contacted me, after you'd been turned, I made the connection right away between the name on the note and the woman I'd heard. Remember, though, we'd never encountered a vampire before. We didn't know of their existence. So

I thought it was either a coincidence or that I'd made it up. Imagined it. But then my mother sent me an update of our family history for the Carruthers library, and I paged through, and there it was. There *she* was. All the stories. I can't deny it."

"God, Cathryn. I can't believe you didn't tell me about Cape May sooner."

"I'm sorry. That time wasn't exactly something I like to dwell on. Forgive me." Cathryn snapped out the words, and I felt the tension in the room rise. She and Lucas had met in the New Jersey seaside resort and had a brief, intense affair. When Cathryn had broken it off abruptly weeks later, Lucas hadn't known why and had assumed Cathryn had simply had a change of heart. I wondered now if what Veronica had said that night that might have caused the break-up.

Lucas ran a hand through his hair. "Okay. Fine. What does this mean?"

"It means that most likely your changing wasn't random or an accident. It means she targeted you, and we don't know whether she did it for good or for ill. But if we could get hold of her, make contact, maybe we'd know more about how you can work with us. And what your destiny holds."

"Fine. I'll just call her and ask. Oh, wait, we have no idea where she is or how to make contact. Gee, thanks for all that help, Cathryn." Lucas almost growled.

"This is a start. I have agents working on finding her, and I promise, we'll figure it out. Now we have a reliable physical description." She swallowed. "I truly am sorry I didn't tell you sooner, Lucas. I thought it had to be coincidence, even though everything in life has convinced me such a thing doesn't exist."

"Don't keep anything like this from me again. Are we clear? Because if you do and I find out, I'm done. Done with Carruthers and done with you."

Cathryn stood up, her face shuttering closed again. "I understand. And I've taken up enough of your time." She reached out to touch my arm, taking me by surprise yet again. She wasn't one for casual affection. "Good luck with the pie contest today."

I raised my eyebrows. "How did you know about that?"

She smiled a little. "Oh, I have my ways. I hear things, you know." For a minute, I thought she might wink at me. "I'll be in touch with both of you. Good-bye."

Chapter 11

"WHAT THE HELL is that supposed to be?"

I recognized Bitsy's voice floating across the tent to me. I'd just arrived and placed my entry on the judging table. Turning, I let my smile grow wider.

"Hello, Bitsy. Happy Triple P Festival. How are you today?"

"That's not a pecan pie." She pointed at my pie and snarled.

"Well, yes, it is. And incidentally, it's the *winning* pecan pie."

Her eyes narrowed. "I guess we'll see." She wheeled around and stomped from the tent.

For a moment, I indulged in a fantasy where today, here at the Festival, it was revealed that Bitsy was the person who'd poisoned Maddy and Trina and killed Dell. In my scenario, there was some vague motive, and she was hauled off by the police just after her pie lost to mine. All the loose ends tied up in a pretty bow—no, make that a ribbon. A shiny blue ribbon.

Sadly, I was pretty sure that theory had a ton of holes. First of all, to my knowledge Bitsy had no motive at all. She probably didn't even know Crissy. Second, poison didn't seem like Bitsy's style. She seemed more the type to shoot a person on Main Street in the middle of the day.

But it was a pleasant thought.

"Hey, was that the bitch?" Nichelle came into the tent, struggling to carry little Jack. "I mean—" She glanced down at her son, who was watching her with interest. "The b-i-t-c-h. She nearly ran me over on the way in here."

"Yep, that's Bitsy. She's an angry woman, isn't she?"

"Just a little. Heyyyyy, look at your pie! Oh, my God, Jackie, it's perfect. Genius. What gave you the idea?"

I thought about my conversation with Mrs. Colby and smiled. "I'm pretty sure it was Al."

Nichelle gave me a side hug. "He'd be so proud of you. When are they announcing the winner?"

"In about an hour or so. The tasting and judging are starting in a minute. Are you sticking around?"

She hoisted the baby higher on her hip. "Of course. Wouldn't miss it. But I think I'll grab the stroller and walk this kiddo around a little bit while we're waiting."

My nerves were stretched so tight, between anticipation

of the pie contest and worry over Lucas, who was at the performance tent already, that I couldn't stand still. I paced the grounds for forty-five minutes, and by the time I got back to the pie judging tent, it was nearly standing room only. I pushed my way to the front, checking out the competition on the table.

There were about thirty pies, I estimated. Each of them was picture-perfect, and I began to second-guess myself. Why had I taken this risk? Why hadn't I stayed safe, following the basic recipe and hoping for the best? I was so screwed. I'd be laughed out of the contest, and no matter what Mary had said, I'd let down everyone at Leone's. Bitsy would gloat, and I'd have to listen to her for a year.

"May I have your attention, please?" A petite woman with curled gray hair stood at the microphone in the front of the tent, beaming at the crowd. "Welcome to the Eighty-Fifth Annual Perfect Pecan Pie Festival! We're just so tickled to have such a wonderful turnout for the announcement of our winning pies. And look at these beautiful entries!" She spread her hand wide, gesturing to the table.

"We'll get to the winners in a moment, but first, we want to thank the lovely Belinda Casey Colby for honoring us with her presence today. Mrs. Colby is the granddaughter of our own beloved General Casey, a part-time resident of Palm Dunes herself, and we are just thrilled to have her here!"

Applause roared in the small space, as Mrs. Colby stood and gave a little bow. I grinned, thinking of Al.

"And now, with no further ado, the winners of the Perfect Pecan Pie Festival! May I have all the entrants come up front, please, so that we can recognize everyone's hard work?"

Most of us were already standing by the table, but a few more people emerged from the crowd, all of them looking as nervous as I felt.

"All right now. Third place goes to . . . Jared Paulson, with his Caramel Crunch Pecan Pie. Congratulations, Jared!"

A guy who was probably in his early thirties stepped forward, accepted the ribbon, and lifted it high over his head to the polite clapping of the audience.

"Quiet now, everyone. Second place goes to . . ." My stomach clenched. "Lacey Robinson, with her Apple Pecan Pie!"

There was more applause as an older lady toddled to the podium and bowed to the judges. Taking her ribbon, she clasped it in both hands and began to speak.

"So honored! Such a wonderful surprise. I have so many people I'd like to thank . . ."

I didn't know whether she'd misunderstood what place she'd won or just felt second prize gave her the right to make a speech, but she was going for it. Several of the officials tried to subtly move her away from the podium, but she wasn't going to be rushed. I giggled, and for the first time, I looked out over the gathering of people waiting for the final announcement.

In one corner of the tent, I spotted Mary, along with several of the servers and the cook from Leone's. Mary caught my eye and gave me a thumb's up. Not too far from them, Crissy Darwin and her parents were trying to be inconspicuous as they watched. Across the tent, the Golden Rays contingent, headed up by Mrs. Mac, were all sending me a variety of encouraging hand signals. Near the tent door, Nichelle stood, holding small

Jack up so that he could see. And a few feet away from them was Lucas, whose eyes never left me.

A lump rose in my throat. These were my people, my tribe. Each one of them was part of me, and I couldn't imagine my life without them. In that moment, I felt Al near me, felt his presence more tangibly than I had since he'd passed. And I realized that this was the legacy he'd left me. It wasn't the pie recipe or winning the contest or even Leone's. It was his sense of community. The way he'd connected with people, made them feel important, loved and wanted. The way he'd listened to us, celebrated our wins and consoled us in our losses. It was how he'd lived, and it was what he was teaching me still. Tears blurred my vision.

"All right, ladies and gentlemen, sorry for the delay. The winner of the Eighty-Fifth Perfect Pecan Pie Festival is . . . Jackie O'Brien with her Florida-Georgia Key Lime Pecan Pie!"

By the time I finished receiving the congratulations of everyone in the tent—everyone, that is, other than Bitsy who'd stomped off, growling—it was nearly time for Crissy's performance. I hugged Nichelle good-bye, since she had to head home with the baby, and waved to the Leone's crowd before I made my way to the front of the tent again.

"Well done, young lady." Mrs. Colby stood near me, beaming. "I'm very proud of you."

"Thank you, Mrs. Colby. You were the inspiration, you know."

"That's kind of you. Tell me how you came up with the idea, exactly. It's quite unique, isn't it?"

I smiled. "It was when you said the General wanted Palm Dunes to be the best of Georgia and Florida. I thought that key limes are the quintessential Florida dessert fruit, and marrying them to pecans seemed to make sense." I reached for my pie and cut a generous slice. "And then I went a step further. I incorporated my grandmother's crust, because it really is the best, and my aunt's basic pecan pie recipe, so it's the best of *my* worlds, too."

"Genius, my dear. I would very much like that recipe, if you don't mind." She handed me a small ivory card. "This is my telephone number. Call me, please, and we'll arrange to have tea. I think we should become better acquainted. I have a feeling we could be good friends."

"I'd like that. It would be my pleasure." I waited until Mrs. Colby had wandered away and then I turned to one of the officials standing behind the table. "May I take this slice of pie and borrow a paper plate? I need to make a delivery."

"Of course. It's your pie, after all." He smiled.

"Thank you." I gathered the slice of pie, snagged a plastic fork from the table and hurried out of the tent and across the Festival to the performance tent.

It was already filled nearly to capacity, but I managed to make my way along the edge to the stage, where several burly men guarded the entrance to backstage.

"Hi, there." I put on a bright smile. "I'm a friend of Crissy's. Oh, and my boyfriend Lucas is playing guitar for her tonight."

They both looked at me skeptically.

I lifted the plate of pie. "I'm bringing Crissy pie."

Now they looked less skeptical and more alarmed. "No way, ma'am. No food brought in."

Damn. I mentally kicked myself. Of course they wouldn't let me bring it in, not when people were being poisoned.

"Hey, guys, this is my girlfriend. She's okay." Lucas must've heard my voice, as he stuck his head through the curtained doorway.

"But she can't bring in the food." The taller of the two men crossed his arms over his massive chest.

"I promise, no one will eat it. We're about to go on, anyway. You have my word."

The guards grudgingly allowed me to pass, and I smiled at Lucas. "Thanks. How're you feeling? Are you ready to rock and roll?"

He shrugged. "It's folk music, so maybe not so much rocking. But we'll definitely roll."

"You're going to knock 'em dead." I hugged him and then stood back, looking up into his face as he winced. "Ooops, sorry. Bad choice of words. You'll wow them."

"Sounds good." He rubbed his hand over his jaw, and I could feel his dancing nerves.

"Jackie!" Crissy wandered over to me. "Congratulations. You must be so happy." I saw the traces of shadows beneath her eyes, only partially covered by makeup. I knew tonight wouldn't be easy for her.

"Thanks." I lifted the plate. "You can't eat this now, of course, but I wanted to carry on Al's tradition. A slice of the winning pie."

"Oh, you remembered." Tears sparkled in her eyes. "Thank you. I'll have it after we get finished tonight. Do me a favor, though, and stay with it the whole time, so I don't have to have it tested first." She rolled her eyes to the watchful man in the corner. "My dad's doing the food monitoring, making sure no one eats anything that hasn't been checked out."

"Of course." I gave her a hug. "Good luck tonight."

"Thanks. Want to watch from back here? You won't have to deal with getting jostled by the crowd."

"A backstage seat? Sure. Thanks."

The lights dimmed, and we heard a man on the stage announcing rising folk music star Crissy Darwin with her guest guitarist, Lucas Reilly. Crissy shot Lucas one last encouraging look and offered him her hand as they walked onto the stage.

I found a folding chair and sat down out of sight of the audience. Lucas was perched on a stool, appearing amazingly relaxed and comfortable as he played the guitar. Crissy stood in the spotlight, in front of the microphone, her voice sweet and strong.

After the first number ended, I balanced the pie plate on my knee while I applauded. Crissy thanked her fans for their support in the wake of the events of the past week, and then she cleared her throat.

"We're really grateful tonight that Lucas Reilly stepped

in to help us by playing guitar. Let's give him a big round of applause for being so willing to join me at the last minute."

Polite clapping swelled and then subsided.

"But I've got to mention someone we're all missing here tonight, someone we're going to miss forever. My guitarist, my first accompanist, Dell Jamison, left us this week." She paused, and I could see she was struggling not to cry. "Dell was a quiet man, and not many people knew him well, but he was a gentleman. He had a wonderful sense of humor, and he always had my back. We don't know for sure, but I believe he died because he was always looking out for me. Dell—"

"BITCH!"

From the other side of the stage, a blurred figure raced toward Crissy, screaming all the while. "You bitch! You never loved him. You took him from me, took my one true love. *I* was the one who loved him, but you stood between us."

I jumped to my feet, just as I recognized the woman. It was Crissy's fan Diane, the woman we'd met in Crystal Cove. She was standing next to the singer, yelling at the top of her lungs. Lucas had stood up, too, and was moving toward the two woman. But something else caught my eye, something in Diane's hand.

It was a knife.

With a shout, I sprinted onto the stage just as Diane raised her arm over Crissy. Lucas, being closer, grabbed the lunatic's arm, but she shook him off and slashed at him. He took one staggering step back, and Diane lifted the knife again.

I'd never played sports in high school. I was more of the journalist, the yearbook writer, the library aid. I didn't like the physical stuff. I wasn't competitive.

But now, with every fiber of my being, every bit of my strength, I threw my body onto Diane, knocking her to the ground. In my mind's eye, she should've dropped the knife when I tackled her, but it didn't quite work out that way. Instead, she screeched at me and struck out.

A stinging sensation bit into my upper arm, but I didn't let go of her. I leaned on her with all of my weight, screwing shut my eyes as she continued to scream and rant.

It seemed like a lifetime before strong arms lifted me from her body, but it was actually only a few seconds. My burly friends, the ones so worried about little old me going backstage, had finally managed to reach us. One of them supported my weight while the other hauled Diane to her feet and held her arms. She never stopped babbling.

"My God, Jackie. Are you okay?" Lucas pulled me into his arms, holding me close to him. The guard stepped away and went to help his partner who was struggling to get Diane under control.

"Yeah, I'm . . . damn, I think I smushed Crissy's pie." I craned my neck to see my chair, where the paper plate lay turned upside down. "Aww, it's ruined now."

"Baby, you were . . . oh, my God, Jackie. You're bleeding." Lucas held up his hand, wet with blood. "She must've stabbed you."

"Wow. Look at that. Blood." I managed to slur out the words and then fainted dead away.

"So it was Diane the whole time?" I glanced at Lucas who was sitting next to me as the EMT's tended to my stab wound. I kept my face in the opposite direction so I could pretend whatever they were doing was happening to someone else. I'd convinced them that I didn't need a trip to the hospital, as long as they could stitch me up here and give me a tetanus shot.

He sighed. "So it seems. From what I can understand, she and Dell had a fling a while back. She fell in love with him, and apparently, he blew her off. She wouldn't take no, so he told her he was in love with Crissy and that was why he couldn't be with her."

"Was he?" Dell hadn't seemed to me to be carrying a torch for the younger woman.

Lucas shrugged. "Who knows? Crissy says no. She thinks Dell just wanted to get rid of Diane and used Crissy as a handy excuse. She says they were always more like brother and sister, but I guess we'll never be sure."

"But she poisoned Maddy?"

"Yeah. She had her hair in a baseball cap and wore a hoodie, and she intercepted the food delivery at the office. She put in the poison on the way up to Maddy, knowing that it was always Crissy who ate the Kung Pao. And at Crystal Cove, she managed to get some of the strychnine into the chili, but not enough—lucky for Trina—because one of the cooks at the

Riptide was watching her."

"But Dell suspected."

"Dell knew her better than anyone else did. And he was the only one who could guess why she'd have motive. That's likely why he didn't tell anyone else—he was embarrassed about using Crissy as a way to shake off Diane. He called her, told her she needed to come forward and confess or he'd go to the cops himself. She went over to his house, argued with him, and then when the fight moved outside—he was heading to the car, to force her to the police station—she grabbed an ax from a stump and killed him."

"My God." I breathed the words. "Poor Dell."

"Yeah." Lucas held my hand, wincing as much as I did while they stitched my arm.

"How did Diane get onstage? They weren't going to let me back until you intervened."

"Good question. She slipped past the guard, who apparently was watching Crissy instead of the doorway. I have a feeling he's not going to be in personal security much longer."

"You tried to stop her, too. Did she hurt you?" I remembered Lucas stumbling back, away from the knife.

"She nicked me a little. Nothing big, and yes, I had it looked at." He kissed my knuckles. "But you're the real hero. You saved Crissy and me, you managed to subdue a crazed killer, and you won the Perfect Pecan Pie Festival."

I lifted the shoulder not being worked on. "All in a day's work."

Lucas held my hand to his face. "But you scared the shit of me. For the second time in two weeks. Don't do that again, okay? I love you. I'm pretty sure I can't live without you. Don't make me try."

"I'll do my best." I bit my lip. "Lucas, can you do me a favor?"

"Anything, baby." He brushed a kiss on the inside of my wrist.

"Can you get me a piece of pie?"

Chapter 12

IT WAS THE perfect Florida autumn evening. There was just enough cool in the breeze that I was glad for my jeans and sweatshirt, and the air was filled with the smoky scent of a nearby bonfire and roasting pecans.

Lucas was still talking with police, but once they'd let me go, I'd needed to get out of the tent. It was claustrophobic and cloying, with too many people in too small a space. Crissy and her parents couldn't stop thanking me, over and over. It was embarrassing. Curious onlookers kept trying to peek through the flaps, and the cops stationed at the openings were getting exasperated with shooing them away. I'd whispered to Lucas that I was going to walk the Festival for a bit, and I'd see him when he was finished.

The lights from the booths and stands danced in the breeze, casting weird shadows as they moved. I shivered just a little, and it wasn't from the cold. In the last ten days, I'd been so preoccupied with all things pie and of course with the murders that I'd pushed to the back of my mind thoughts of what we'd learned about the coming battle, at least until Cathryn's visit this afternoon had brought it roaring back. Lucas and I hadn't said much about that conversation after she left, both of us focused on our respective challenges: mine the pie contest, and his performing with Crissy.

Now, though, here in the dark, even in the relative safety of the crowd, I couldn't help thinking about it.

Fighting an evil that had been planning this war for decades, maybe even eons, terrified me. What I'd seen in Diane's eyes tonight had been scary, sure. But it was madness, not evil. She was crazy. The idea that Lucas and all the other Carruthers agents might have to risk everything in the approaching storm clutched at my stomach, making it hard to breathe. All of them . . . Rafe, Nell, even Cathryn . . . they were my friends. I couldn't imagine knowing they were walking into danger.

And Lucas. There was no way I'd stand back and let him fight. I wanted to protect him, take him away and hide until it was all over and the battle was decided. I knew my boyfriend was capable of defending himself. He was strong and brave, and he'd go forward without hesitation. But part of me worried that he wasn't ready. Nell and Rafe and Cathryn . . . they'd had their abilities their entire lives. Their power was great, and they knew how to use it. Lucas was still figuring how who and what he was. It wasn't safe.

I couldn't lose him. Panic gripped me, and my heart pounded. I loved this man with every ounce of my being, and I'd do anything to keep him safe, even if it meant risking my own life. Even if it meant letting Delia or any other spirit possess me again. I shuddered, wrapping my arms around my waist.

"Oh, excuse me." The voice was musical, almost other-worldly, and the face that came with it was so beautiful, I nearly gasped. Her hair was black silk, cascading around slim shoulders, but it was the eyes that stole my breath . . . they were gorgeous. Ice-blue, they felt a little familiar, like seeing a face I recognized in the wrong setting.

"I didn't mean to bump into you." She spoke again, and I was mesmerized. "Too preoccupied with watching all the pretty lights, I guess."

Her words held a touch of accent, but I couldn't pinpoint exactly where it was from. European, certainly; not quite French, not exactly Spanish . . . Italian? No, she didn't sound like Al or like my Nonna, both who'd had a touch of the Old Country in their voices.

"That's all right." I smiled. "I know what you mean. I was just thinking how lovely everything looks, and what a perfect evening this is."

"Very true." Her lips curved, and she leaned forward just slightly, her head drawing near mine, almost as though she was . . . breathing me in. A warning chill zipped down my spine, and I shifted away.

As thought I'd imagined her movement, she continued speaking. "Your Festival is very charming."

"Thank you." I inclined my head in acknowledgement. "You're not from this area, I take it?"

She laughed, and it sounded like bells ringing. "No, I'm not. I have . . . family in Florida, however. I've enjoyed exploring it. It's a very interesting state."

"It is." I didn't know what else to say, and the silence stretched close to awkwardness before she reached to touch my arm, where the bandage the EMTs had applied still covered my wound.

"What's this? Have you hurt yourself?"

I shook my head. "It was nothing. A little accident, but it's better now. Mostly."

She tilted her head. "Aren't you the person who won the pie contest? Congratulations. Your entry was innovative."

"Thanks. Did you try any of it?"

"Sadly, no." She lifted one shoulder in a very Gallic shrug. "I don't indulge in sweets."

"Well, I admire your discipline. I have absolutely none."

"I wouldn't say that." Her smile widened. "I think there may be more to you than meets the eye, Jackie."

"Ah, I only meant when it came to desserts." My smile faded a little. *Had she just called me by my name?* I hadn't introduced myself—but then, there was the pie contest. She must've seen my name by my entry or heard the announcement. That was surely it.

"I'm glad I had the chance to speak with you." She looked over my shoulder, beyond me into the crowd, and her eyes flared for the space of a breath. "If you'll excuse me, I'm meeting friends, and I don't want to be late."

"Oh, sure, nice talking with you. Enjoy the Festival."

With a quick wave, she moved away from me, and within seconds, vanished into the crowd. I felt that same chill, the shiver that ran over me.

"Who was that? Talking to you?"

I jumped as Lucas grabbed my shoulder from behind, his fingers digging into my skin. "That lady? I don't know. She—"

"Where did she go?"

"I have no idea. To meet friends, she said. Why?" I turned and looked up into his face, cupping his cheek with my hand.

Lucas closed his eyes. Beneath my palm, his skin had gone clammy and pale. He drew in a shuddering breath before he spoke.

"That's the woman who turned me into a vampire."

The End
For Now

Rafe and Nell Go To The Beach

Earlier this year, the kind people at Literary Escapism asked me to write a short post about two of my characters at the beach. That seemed an easy task, since I was in the middle of releasing three books, all set at the beach. But it seemed a little too simple to write about the people of Crystal Cove at the beach. So I decided instead to write about The Couple Least Likely to Go To The Beach: Nell and Rafe.

Of course, when they did go to the beach, they ended up in Crystal Cove, which worked out well, since that place and those people are near and dear to me.

I decided to include this little piece here, since Rafe and Nell both reference the visit when they meet Jackie and Lucas in Crystal Cove.

If you want to read more about Crystal Cove, there are three books in that series, with more on the way: ***The Posse, The Plan*** *and* ***The Path****.*

If you want to read more about Rafe and Nell, check out ***Undeniable*** *and* ***Unquenchable****, as well as* ***The Shadow Bells, a Serendipity Short****.*

And if you'd like some more background on Cathryn and Lucas, pre-Jackie, you'll want to read ***Stardust on the Sea, a Serendipity and Recipe for Death Short****.*

Finally, if you want to read what happened at Carruthers right before ***Death A La Mode*** *began, the short story* ***Unforgettable*** *is included in the anthology* ***It's A Ghoul Thing****.*

The following appeared originally on the blog Literary Escapism on August 28, 2015 (http://www.literaryescapism.com/).

"I'M NOT GOING to the beach."

I didn't even bother turning around to check out Rafe's expression. I knew what it would be: a mix of patient exasperation and frustration, the same way he looked whenever I dug in my heels about something he wanted me to do. I waited for his next move, which was typically a sigh as he came up behind me and slid his arms around my waist, pulling me tight against his hard body and began to persuade me in his own special way.

But this time, he didn't move. When I finally turned around to sneak a peek at what he was doing, his head was bent over the slim silver laptop on the counter in front of him. He wasn't even looking my way. I frowned.

Rafe's eyes didn't leave the computer screen, and his fingers flew over the keys. If he'd heard me, he wasn't giving any indication of it. I slammed the door of the coffee mug cabinet, and finally he glanced up at me, his green eyes distracted.

"Did you hear me? I said I'm not going to the beach."

He lifted one shoulder in a shrug. "Okay."

Okay? Since when had my boyfriend—yes, I still winced at the use of that word, but what else could I call Rafe? My lover? My roommate? My screwing buddy? Since all of my limited circle knew the deal about our relationship, I rarely had to use that word, but sometimes among strangers or acquaintances, it slipped out. But since when had he given into me so easily when I gave him a hard time? My stomach clenched as old insecurities flooded back.

"Okay, as in we're not going to do it, or okay, as in you're still going to go?" I leaned back against the counter and crossed my arms over my chest.

"Okay, as in I made the commitment for us to go, and even if you don't, I am. I promised Cathryn we'd take care of it."

I made a face. "Why can't someone else handle it? She has a whole institute of people at her disposal."

"Everyone else is busy or on assignment. It's not as if it's a challenging job, Nell. It's a possibly haunted hotel in a small beach town a couple of hours away. Cathryn offered it to us as a favor. She figured we could combine business with . . . pleasure." Now he did shut the computer and advance around the kitchen island toward me, a predatory gleam in his eyes. "The beach is supposed to be a romantic setting, you know. Sunsets over clear blue water, the lapping of the waves against the soft white sand, the heat of the sun . . ."

"Sand getting into inconvenient places, blistering sunburns on my very pale skin . . . and the sun doesn't set on that coast, it rises on that side."

This time Rafe did sigh as he grabbed my hand and tugged me close, wrapping both arms around me. "Nell, how many times do I really ask you to do anything you don't want to do?"

I burrowed my face against his chest, breathing in pure Rafe, the one drug that calmed me, body and soul. "Well, there was Christmas a few years back—"

"Uh huh, and did I tell you that we had to go back to King? No, I suggested that we go to Nebraska and make like snow bunnies."

I rolled my eyes. "But I did go."

"Yes, and I really appreciated it. Didn't I show you that?" He nuzzled my neck, his tongue darting out to touch the pulse there. "C'mon, Nell. I just want to lie on the beach with my beautiful girlfriend and veg a little. I promise, you don't have to socialize or anything. Just go for me."

I heaved out a deep breath. "Fine. I'll go to the beach. But I won't like it."

* * *

I liked the beach.

I didn't want to like it. I wanted to sit there wrapped in layers of my gauzy cover-up, brooding. But I couldn't, not when the sun was beaming down on us, and a soft breeze cooled our skin. Not when Rafe peeled off his shirt and his tan skin gleamed against the white of the powder-soft sand.

He dropped onto the blanket he'd carefully spread for me, moving over until his hip bumped mine, and wrapped his arm around my shoulders. "Now this isn't too bad, is it?"

I raised one eyebrow. "Hmm. Not so far. But wait until people get here."

"It's September, baby. We're going to have this beach to ourselves."

And he was right. Oh, a few people strolled by, walking with their feet in the surf. A couple of joggers passed us. But for the most part, it was deserted and quiet and—perfect.

When my stomach began to rumble around noon, Rafe stood up and pulled me to my feet. "We can leave our blanket here and go grab some burgers up at the Riptide. No one's going to bother them."

I glanced down, dubious. "Are you sure?" The aroma of grilled meat began to waft over us, and suddenly I was ravenous. "How do you know this place is any good?"

A shadow passed over his face, fleeting but undeniable. "I ate here once before. On my way to Savannah."

I knew then, and I swallowed hard. He'd have been here with Joss, his partner and lover, on their way to the assignment that would take her life and nearly kill Rafe, too. I remembered those dark days in the aftermath of his rescue, when he'd tried to convince me to let him die.

We didn't talk about Joss much these days, but her ghost could reappear any time, a reminder of how much he'd loved her during their brief relationship. I was hardly the poster child for self-assurance when it came to Rafe and me, but most of the time, I held my own. I couldn't fight against a dead girl, though.

"It's okay, Nell." He ran one finger down the side of my face, brushing away a strand of my black hair. "It's just a memory. It's not real and alive, like you. Let's go enjoy some burgers."

I gave him my hand, and we trudged through the sand to the steps of the wooden deck of the beach-front restaurant. We had our pick of tables, and Rafe pulled out a chair for me at one near the railing, so we could look out over the ocean.

"It's pretty here." The admission didn't come easily. "I never thought I'd be a beach girl, but maybe I can be re-formed."

"Nell, baby." He rubbed his thumb over my knuckles, and warmth flooded me at his use of the endearment. We weren't a cuddly couple who called each "sweetie" or "honeybunch". In bed sometimes, he'd slip and call me "babe", but I knew right now, he was reaching out, trying to soothe me. "You can be anyone you want to be. I love you whether or not you enjoy the beach. How I feel about you doesn't depend on sand or surf."

A door opened from the restaurant's main building, and a pretty woman with hair as dark as mine stepped out, heading our way.

Rafe squeezed my hand. "Oh, by the way . . . we're meeting our contact here. That's her, I'd guess."

I bit back a sharp response. Rafe knew me too well sometimes. I'd have bitched and stressed over meeting someone new if given the time, but now, all I could do was paste on the closest thing to a smile and do the job.

Her eyes flickered between us as she approached, and her lips curved on one side.

"Hello. I'm Abby Donavan, and I think we may have a ghost in my hotel."

Good Night, Travel Well The Killers

Here Today Paul McCartney

Don't Fear The Reaper Blue Oyster Cult

Afterlife Avenged Sevenfold

Getting Late Rob Thomas

Another Day Tim O'Brien

Here Nor There Sarah Jarosz

Those Days Are Gone, and My Heart is Breaking Barton Carroll

Jackie's Florida-Georgia Key Lime Pecan Pie

Winner of the Perfect Pecan Pie Festival

1 cup pecans, chopped
2/3 cup sugar
1 cup cane sugar syrup
4 eggs
2 TBS butter, melted
1 tsp vanilla
1 tsp key lime zest, plus extra for garnish
5 egg yolks
1 can sweetened condensed milk (14 ounces)
½ cup Key Lime juice

For garnish:
1 cup heavy whipping cream
3 TBS confectioners' sugar
1 tsp vanilla

Prepared Pie Crust (see Nana's Perfect Pie Crust)

Preheat the oven to 425 degrees.

Beat the 4 eggs until frothy. Add sugar, cane syrup, vanilla, melted butter and mix well. Stir in pecans. Pour mixture into prepared pie crust in pan. Place on a cookie sheet and bake in preheated oven for 35 minutes.

While the pecan layer is baking, grate the Key Limes for 1 tsp of zest. Beat the egg yolks well, and then add sweetened condensed milk until well-blended. Add the Key Lime juice and the zest. Mix until blended.

Remove pie from oven and lower oven temperature to 350 degrees.

Pour Key Lime mixture over the pecan layer. Return to the oven for 15 minutes. Cool on a wire rack before adding garnish.

Garnish: In a chilled bowl, using a chilled beater, mix the heavy whipping cream at a rapid speed. After about 3 minutes, slowly add the powdered sugar while mixing. When stiff peaks begin to form, add the vanilla. Continue beating until desired consistency is reached. Add a dollop to the center and pipe a line of whipped cream around the edge. Add whole pecans and Key Lime zest as desired.

Nana's Perfect Pie Crust

2 cups flour
½ tsp sugar
¼ tsp salt
½ tsp baking powder
1 cup shortening
1 egg
1 tsp vinegar

Sift together dry ingredients. (Must we sift anymore, with pre-sifted flour? I don't know, but I do it because that's how Nana did it, and besides, sifting is fun. It's like making a snow storm.) Cut shortening into dry ingredients. Break the egg into a measuring cup, then fill up with water to make ½ cup. Add vinegar and then pour into flour/shortening mix. Combine with a wooden spoon and then if necessary, with your hands, but do not over-handle. Roll out to make 2-3 14-inch crusts.

Al's Prize-Winning Pecan Pie Recipe

From the files of Belinda Casey Colby

I wasn't going to tell that dear child, but Al entrusted me with his recipe the year before he died. He told me that he didn't want it falling into the wrong hands should something happen to him—which it did, of course, so that was quite forward-thinking of him. He asked me to add it to the small museum I'm putting together in the General's honor and memory.

Here it is. Enjoy. But please don't tell Jackie. She's finding her own way now.

½ cup white sugar
½ cup brown sugar
3 TBS butter, melted
½ cup cane syrup
3 eggs, beaten
2 TBS bourbon
1 cup chopped spiced pecans (recipe for spicing below)
Prepared pie crust

Preheat an oven to 375 degrees. Mix the white sugar, brown sugar, and butter. Stir in the cane syrup, eggs and bourbon; add the pecans. Pour the mixture into the pie crust. Bake in the preheated oven for 10 minutes then reduce heat to 350 degrees F. Continue to bake about 25 minutes. Allow to cool completely before serving.

Spiced Pecans

1 lb shelled pecans
1 egg white
1 TBS water
1 cup sugar
1 tsp cinnamon
1 tsp salt

Place egg white and water in large bowl and beat until frothy. Add nuts and stir gently until all are covered. Mix Sugar cinnamon and salt. Stir in gently until all nuts are covered. placed nuts on a large lightly greased cookie sheet. Bake in preheated oven at 300 degrees for 30-40 minutes, stirring every 10 minutes. DO NOT OVER BAKE. Transfer nuts to clean, dry cookie sheet to cool.

Acknowledgments

I'm a huge believer that everything happens for a reason. If you saw me this year at any event and asked if I were releasing any paranormal novels, I probably told you no. Because I didn't intend to do it. This was supposed to the year of the contemporary romance.

But then I was invited to participate in a Halloween anthology, and the short had to be paranormal. As it began to take shape, I realized that I might as well write Lucas and Jackie's next installment, too; it made sense on many levels. However, I hadn't written a paranormal, single-point-of-view book in over a year, and jumping back into that world was challenging.

I'm definitely glad I did it, as this story moves us closer to what I'm calling in my head The Big Show Down, the confrontation that's been brewing since the beginning of *Fearless* way back when. A few years ago, I promised my son I'd write an apocalyptic book that he could enjoy (read: no sex). The idea for that book came to me in a dream (seriously). The plot sat on a vague spot in the back of my mind, but as I've delved into where Jackie and Lucas and Nell and Rafe—and Cathryn—are going, I realized that story—that apocalyptic tale—is *their* story. It's the book that will reunite Tasmyn, Michael and their families with Rafe and Nell. Jackie, Lucas and Cathryn will be playing big parts, too. Look for that book in 2017.

Okay, on to the gratitude. Big thank yous, hugs and mongo bottles of wine to: Kelly Baker, proofreader par excellence, Stacey Blake of Champagne Formats, formatter formidable and beloved friend, Stephanie Nelson of Once Upon A Time Covers, gifted cover designer (everyone LOVES the *Recipe for Death* covers. They're just adorable.) and Maria Clark and Jen Rattie for keeping me organized and promoted. Thank you and a shared glass of wine to Heather Batchelder, who took my new author photos and made me look good!

Hugs, love and appreciation to Mandie Stevens, who loves this series so much and cheers me on, and who also offers savvy promo advice and help.

Much love to my pal and rock partner Olivia Hardin. #NVNG2016.

Kisses thrown to the Naughty Temptresses, who offer me honest opinions, laughs and a place where I can be me. I adore all of you—you make me happy every day!

And last but never ever least, thanks, love, hugs, kisses and giggles to my family, both skin and fur variety. Thank you for not killing me when I growl at you while under deadline. Thanks for understanding about virtual events, and thanks for traipsing the country with me for real-life book cons. Thanks for running to the grocery store, feeding pets, listening to me rant and loving me when I'm unlovable. What more could one wife and mama ask?

About the Author

Photo by Heather Batchelder

Tawdra Kandle writes romance, in just about all its forms. She loves unlikely pairings, strong women, sexy guys, hot love scenes and just enough conflict to make it interesting. Her books run from YA paranormal romance through NA paranormal and contemporary romance to adult contemporary and paramystery romance. She lives in central Florida with a husband, kids, sweet pup and too many cats. And yeah, she rocks purple hair.

Follow Tawdra on Facebook, Twitter, Instagram, Pinterest and sign up for her newsletter (http://tiny.cc/TawdraNewsletter) so you never miss a trick.

If you love Tawdra's books, become a Naughty Temptress! Join the group here (http://tiny.cc/NaughtyTemptresses) for sneak peeks, advanced reader copies of future books, and other fun.

Printed in the USA
CPSIA information can be obtained
at www.ICGtesting.com
JSHW031714140824
68134JS00038B/3689

9 781682 301845